DATE DUE		

OUTWARD BOUND

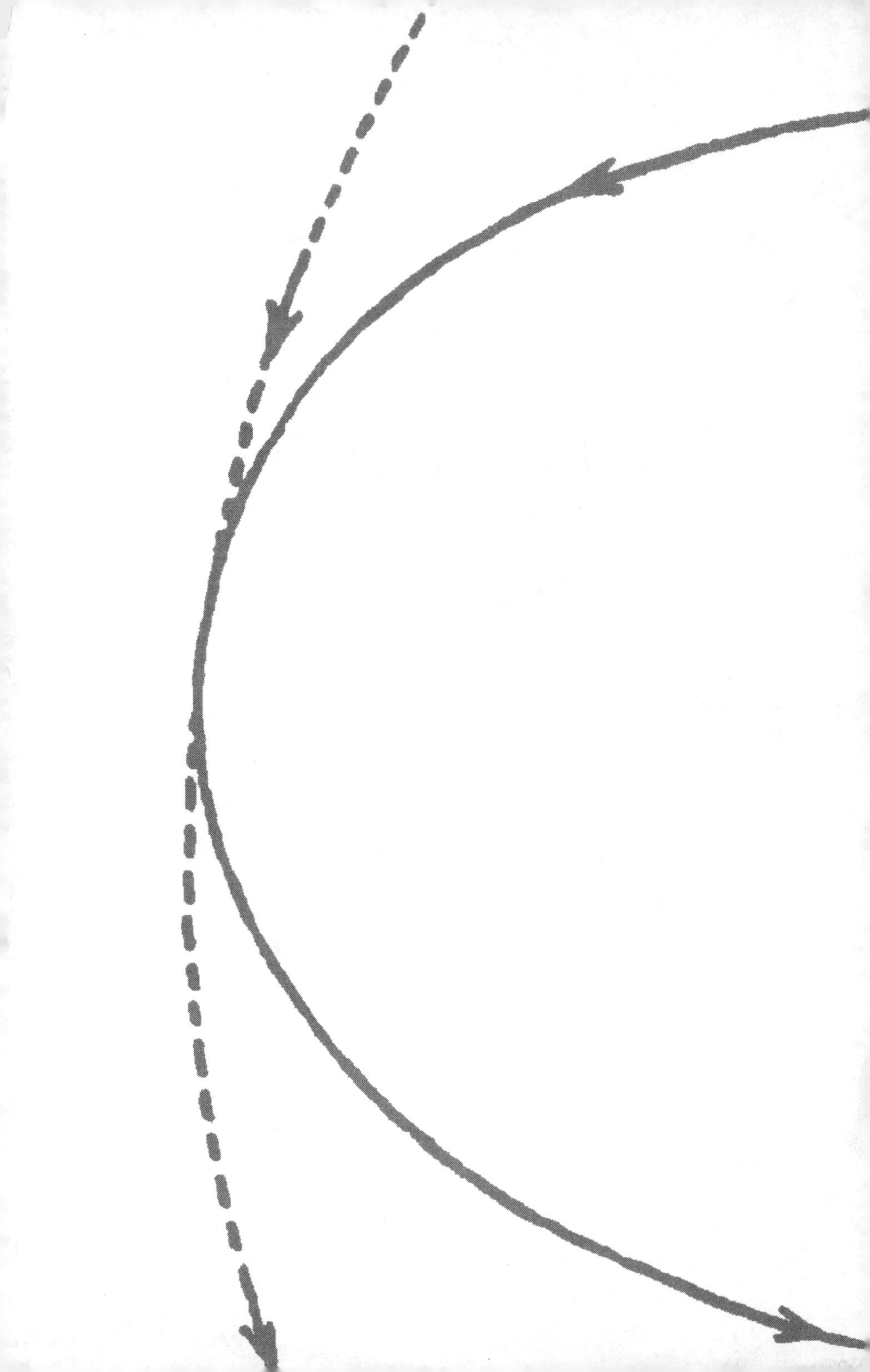

OUTWARD BOUND

A *JUPITER*™ NOVEL

JAMES P. HOGAN

A TOM DOHERTY ASSOCIATES BOOK • NEW YORK

This is a work of fiction. All the characters and events portrayed in this novel are either fictitious or are used fictitiously.

OUTWARD BOUND

This book is printed on acid-free paper.

A Tor Book
Published by Tom Doherty Associates, Inc.
175 Fifth Avenue
New York, NY 10010

Tor Books on the World Wide Web:
http://www.tor.com

Library of Congress Cataloging-in-Publication Data

Hogan, James P.
Outward bound / James P. Hogan. — 1st ed.
p. cm.
"A Tom Doherty Associates book."
ISBN 0-312-86243-1
I. Title.
PR6058.O348O98 1999
823'.914—DC21 98-43789
CIP

First Edition: March 1999

Printed in the United States of America

0 9 8 7 6 5 4 3 2 1

To Maggie

OUTWARD BOUND

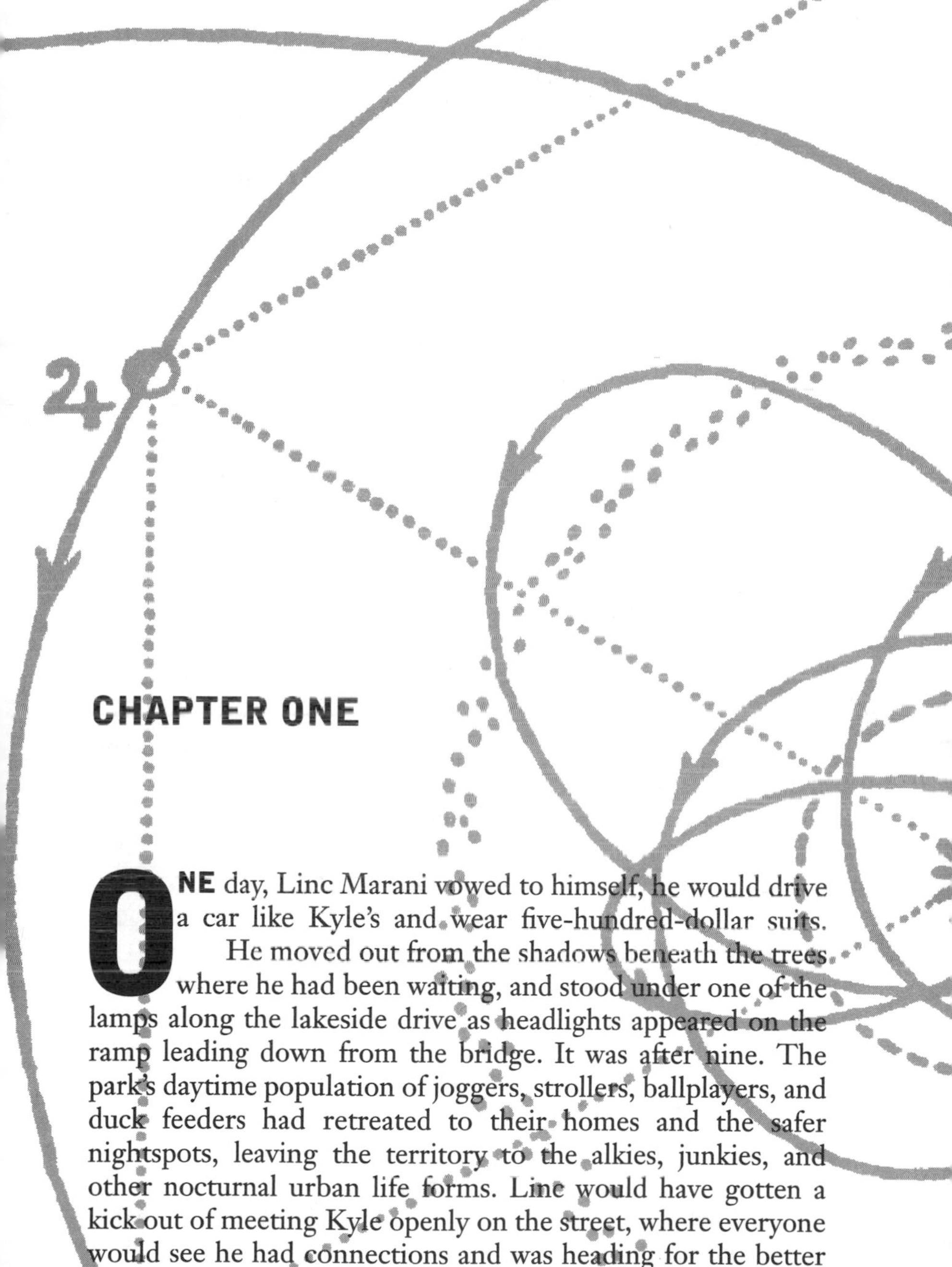

CHAPTER ONE

ONE day, Linc Marani vowed to himself, he would drive a car like Kyle's and wear five-hundred-dollar suits.

He moved out from the shadows beneath the trees where he had been waiting, and stood under one of the lamps along the lakeside drive as headlights appeared on the ramp leading down from the bridge. It was after nine. The park's daytime population of joggers, strollers, ballplayers, and duck feeders had retreated to their homes and the safer nightspots, leaving the territory to the alkies, junkies, and other nocturnal urban life forms. Linc would have gotten a kick out of meeting Kyle openly on the street, where everyone would see he had connections and was heading for the better life. But it couldn't be that way, of course. Some things you just didn't advertise to the world. The first lesson was to be professional. Always professional.

Eighty thousand dollars' worth of Cadillac eased to a halt in front of him, showing white panels and side stripe on pale yellow in the glow from the lamp above. City lights from the far shore reflected in the shine. Kyle Nass lowered the window and rested his elbow on the door, and Linc stooped to bring their faces level. The girl in the passenger seat sent him a cool look that didn't quite mask her curiosity. Linc had a quick impression of a heavily made-up mouth and eyes, hair streaked with blond flashes against hues impossible to distinguish in the shadow.

"So, how ya been?" Kyle opened.

"Oh . . . getting by," Linc answered.

"I got a job that needs doing," Kyle said. "You want some work? We wouldn't want to think of you starting to get hungry out here."

"I do okay. Hey, if it's something that needs doing. . . ." Linc turned a palm. "That's good enough."

Kyle looked away to talk to the girl. "See what I mean? Dedicated. This is Linc. He's gonna be a great soldier one day. Linc, say hello to Mitzi. She's the new light of my life. Ain't she really something, though, huh?"

Linc peered past him to take in the red leather coat thrown open, revealing a low-cut white top, barely clinging to the ends of ample, outthrust breasts. He nodded expressionlessly, complying with Kyle's request but offering nothing anyone could take exception to. "Hi."

"So, we have business? Okay, let's talk." Kyle climbed out from the car, letting Linc close the door for him, and crossed the riverside walk to the water's edge. Linc followed. The yellow waves of Kyle's hair bowed as he paused to light a cigarette, his features illuminated briefly. He blew a stream of smoke into the night and resumed in a lowered voice.

"We've got an overdue collection for two grand. The mark is a spick who goes as Gabriel Colomada. Fleshy, with a beard, some kind of accountant with habits that eat money, rents in a greaseball apartment house called Amigo's on Twenty-third off

Canal, number C-8. Most Friday and Saturday nights he puts in an appearance at that Irish bar that those two brothers run—a couple of blocks away, on Griffin."

"Cleary's?"

"That's the one. The message needs to be delivered this week."

Linc nodded. "Sure. Nice and clear." He knew the routine.

Kyle reached inside his coat. Gold rings flashed in the lamplight as he produced an envelope. "The Man likes the way you've been operating, Linc. There's a hundred here over the last figure. Same terms. You cover your own expenses."

Linc took the envelope and pocketed it. "The same bonus?" he said, checking.

"Ten percent extra if you collect before Sunday," Kyle confirmed.

"Fine."

"Any other questions?"

Linc shook his head.

"Well, that's just great, kid. You're gonna go far." They walked back to the car.

Mitzi looked across again as Linc held the door open for Kyle to get in, perhaps trying to reconcile the image of a fifteen-year-old, which she had been expecting, with the person she glimpsed outside in the night: muscular frame touching six feet inside a black suede jacket and gray turtleneck; hair cropped short and glistening; not bad looks, but with features hard and unyielding, darkened at the chin and upper lip by stubble already proclaiming the man.

Linc caught her eye as he closed the door. There was an interest there, yet restrained—not quite hidden by the aloofness she was trying to project. *Maybe one day*, the look seemed to say. *Try me again when you've made the grade, kid.*

Damn right, Linc told himself as he watched the Cadillac reverse, turn, and drive away back up the ramp. One day he'd have a chick like *that* in his car too.

CHAPTER TWO

TWO evenings later, in the streets by the river on the South Side, Linc reappeared at the low-rent monument to abandoned delusions that was all his parents had to show for twenty years of drink, drugs, and being suckered into every promise of a quick fix to life's ills that the ad lines had to offer. In the earlier days there had been a succession of "business things" that somebody or other his father knew had gotten going, inevitably with the assurance to his mother that "you won't believe what's gonna happen!"; except that it never quite did somehow, apart from the debts they were left with and another screaming fight that would carry on intermittently for weeks.

Sadie, one of Linc's two older sisters, had left town with a sugar daddy who drove a repo Honda and was going to put her in a penthouse. That had been before the family moved out of the house they'd had off Central. Afterward, the other sister, Marcella, moved in with a creep who fenced electronics and pushed weed in the projects—and whom Linc had once been obliged to visit and "educate" a little after Marcella came home in dark glasses with a swollen mouth and the story that she'd walked into a door. Now only Linc was left to stomp the roaches around the cartons of empties in the kitchen and watch the gaudy furniture coming apart while he served out his time of mandatory social processing masquerading as schooling, to become an aid-program statistic or wage serf on the corporate plantations. At least that was the presumed pattern. Linc Marani, however, had other plans.

His mother was zonked on the couch in the living room with her head in a VR helmet, muttering to herself. Not bothering to rouse her, he went through to the back, showered, and selected a tan zipper jacket and charcoal jeans from his closet. His pocket phone beeped just as he finished changing.

"Yeah?"

"Linc? Clay here."

"What gives?"

Clay and Slam were young muscle from the area, whom Linc had hired as backup for the job. He'd used them before. Clay was black, fast, and mean but liked girls and powder too much to be capable of hanging onto money. Slam wasn't overendowed when it came to smarts, but he followed instructions with the diligence and predictability of a washing machine, and the size of him was sometimes enough to induce quick settlement of an account with no more than a mild reminder on the meaning of punctuality. It was Friday. Linc had left them staking out Cleary's bar. A twenty slipped to the bartender would give them the identification if Colomada appeared.

"The beard just showed, solo," Clay's voice informed. "He's inside now. Slam's watchin' the turf. Seems we've got ourselves a party in the makin' here."

"I'm on my way over," Linc answered. "Call you when I'm on Griffin. Let me know if the scene moves."

"Gotcha."

Linc disconnected and put the phone back inside his jacket. Then he took down a box he kept on the top shelf of the closet, and from it transferred a pair of thick, leather-backed work gloves to one of his pockets, and a set of brass knuckles to the other. He'd never actually had to use the knuckles, since the sight plus the circumstances had always been sufficient to intimidate a victim into "negotiating." And that was just as well. To Linc the work was a ticket up from life's basement level, not something he did for the love of it. Given the choice, he would prefer to do without messiness.

As Linc came out from his room, locking the door, his father appeared in the hallway. He was wearing his expression of exaggerated friendliness that always set Linc's teeth on edge—partly an apology for intruding, partly that inane grin he put on to show he was harmless. *See, I'm not bothering you,* it seemed to say. *Not asking questions. Don't you owe it to like me a little, at least?* It usually meant he wanted a favor.

"Say, Linc, you're back. When did you get in?"

"A while ago."

"Does your mother know you're here?"

"There wasn't any point in telling her. I'm just going back out."

"Oh. . . . Okay." A biting of the lip and an awkward momentary flexing of fingers signaled *how to bring this up before he leaves?* "We, er, had a visit from the school inspector's office. Seems they've been missing you again for a couple of days. . . . I didn't tell 'em anything, though. Said I thought you had personal problems you're having to work out, that might be affecting things." *See how I'm on your side. We can be friends, eh?*

"Okay." Linc shrugged indifferently, looking in the direction of the door.

His father moved a pace closer. "Say, uh . . . something came up, and I didn't get around to cashing my check today. You wouldn't be able to help me out with, say, twenty toward a little drop of something for tonight, would you? Only temporary—till I see Andy tomorrow. . . ."

"Andy's out of town. You know he is, because Marcella called three days ago to ask if we had his number. She said then that he wouldn't be back for a month."

"I can tap George at the deli. He owes me—"

Linc waved the rest aside with a shake of his head and peeled a fifty off a roll he produced from his belt.

"Say, are you sure? . . ." But his father was already reaching for it. "I'll have it back for you by—"

"It doesn't matter. Keep it," Linc said curtly.

And he left before the taste in his mouth could get any worse. Bad luck could happen to anybody, and anyone might be in need of a helping hand one day. But to have no pride. That was something else.

CHAPTER THREE

THE two street hookers regarded him approvingly as he came around the corner from Broad, a block short of Griffin. "Hey, Big Guy, wanna go out tonight? Looking for a good time?"

Linc permitted a smile that stopped short of condescension. "I got business tonight. Maybe later." He didn't mean it. Girls were another thing, like dope and booze, that took over guys' lives and ate into their brains. Not that Linc was opposed to a little fooling around when the opportunity was there and made sense. But it wasn't something you shopped for along the street like some kind of acidhead, cyberzom, or other t-dep being milked by every kind of pusher. It wasn't that the girls were at fault—what else were they doing, after all, but using what they had to get what they could, just as he and the rest of the world did? But when something in that line made a dent in his life, it would be in a situation where there could be a little more respect—both ways.

Respect was a big word in Linc's vocabulary. It meant being selective and paying attention to things that mattered and people who made differences. And respect for oneself meant being valuable enough to make sure they would notice you. That was the key to doing better than just getting by and surviving, which was something even the rats in the sewers under the city managed. The value of kids like Linc to the people Kyle worked for—and whom Linc would work for directly one day—was that their own enforcers were known, filed, cataloged, and watched, and a finger trail put together by a sharp DA with big ideas could bring grief and ruin to some important people. But juveniles enjoyed a wider definition of rights and more fundamental presumptions of innocence, with the attendant risk of conviction ranging from more difficult, at worst, to improbable. And even if a bad hand did turn up, the money was there for attorneys who specialized in bargaining this kind of rap down to minimum or nothing. The best there were. Kyle had said so.

Linc's phone beeped. It was Clay again. "The beard's just comin' back out on the street now. Gotta purple kinda parka and a green hat. Slam's right in there behind him, and I'm closin' after 'em. Headin' your way. You made the Griff yet?"

Even better than planned. Linc wouldn't have to spend time hanging around. "Two blocks along," he responded. "Take it like we said."

"Right on."

Had Colomada gone the other way, Linc would have crossed and overtaken on the far side, then doubled back to intercept them from the opposite direction. As things were, he made fast time along the block of shuttered storefronts, a dingy Chinese restaurant, and a late-night food mart, and then crossed the avenue while Colomada and his two tails were still halfway along the block ahead, coming the other way. The street was darker and emptier here, with locked entrances to dirty office buildings, and garbage Dumpsters standing by a truck-loading dock closed behind heavy steel doors. Past the loading dock an alley opened off to the left, opposite a vacant lot being used for parking.

Pulling on the gloves as he walked, Linc paced himself to approach the alley while keeping the same distance from it as Colomada. At the same time Clay and Slam moved up from behind to flank Colomada on either side. Linc was placed to block him if he sensed something amiss and tried to run.

They all reached the mouth of the alley together. As Clay and Slam drew level with the hunched, shuffling figure, they seized his arms suddenly and changed direction to propel him out of sight off the street.

"*What—*" The beginning of a shout died in a gasp as Linc thudded a solid punch into Colomada's midriff. Colomada slumped back against the wall, arms pinned by the two holding him on either side. Linc hit him several more times to the body—just softening-up blows. With luck, fear would do the rest.

"You've been getting forgetful, Gabriel," Linc said.

Colomada answered in short, heaving bursts. "How . . . you know me? Who are you? . . . I don't know what you talk about."

"I think you do. Some friends of mine are short of somewhere around two thousand dollars. They're getting impatient."

Colomada was breathing shakily. In the glow from the street, Linc could make out his eyes wide and staring, mouth gaping as he fought for air. He slipped on the knuckles, making sure to keep his movements slow and visible in the light.

Something that hadn't felt right should have warned him. Something too stiff and unyielding about Colomada's body when Linc hit it.

Linc didn't see exactly what happened in the darkness, but there was rapid, sudden movement and the sound of blows, and Slam doubled over with a gurgle, clutching his throat. Clay's reflexes kicked in at once and he tried to split, but light flooded the alley and two unmarked cars blocked the end, already disgorging uniformed figures. Linc started to wheel the other way.

"Freeze! Right there!"

He found himself looking at the muzzle of a .45, a Police Department shield being brandished, and the face of a very different, mean and nasty-looking Gabriel Colomada.

Running footsteps; a fleeting impression of Clay spread-eagled against one of the cars; Slam being hauled to his feet, retching and choking. Hands were seizing Linc and shoving.

"Against the wall, punk. Reach up it, high." Pain, as a nightstick struck into his kidney; then being frisked, head jerked back and held by the hair. *"Both hands down and behind your back."* Cuffs jammed on roughly, cutting into his wrists. Lights and sirens. More pushing and shoving, toward one of the cars. . . . A blow from behind sent him staggering into the backseat, causing him to hit his head on the top of the door painfully.

"Hey, Chas, don't get too eager there," someone called out sarcastically. "Don't you know he's only a juvenile? We might have to put you on a refresher for sensitivity training."

"He can file a complaint at the station," Colomada's voice snarled from outside as the door slammed shut.

CHAPTER FOUR

THERE are ways, using wet towels wrapped around the knuckles or blows delivered with other parts of the hand, of working a body over thoroughly without leaving marks that would provide provable grounds for complaint. Linc had experienced the joys of this form of supplementary education the last time he was picked up by the police. His two arrests before that had been when they were called out to the school: first, two days after he was transferred there, when the grade bully tried teaching the new kid the lesson on who was boss and wound up with a wired jaw; and second, when he lost patience with a teacher who wanted to hang equal blame on one of the younger kids for *defending* himself when he got picked on. (Getting rough with a teacher hadn't been really smart, Linc later admitted to himself. They were just stuck with the same stupid rules as everyone else. The problem was, you could never find or get near the people who made them.) On both those occasions he'd ended up being lectured by a counselor who'd probably never been on a street after dark, and had to answer endless dumb questions put by a psychiatrist who assured Linc that none of it was his fault. (*Great*, Linc had thought. *If none of it was his fault, why were they wasting their time with him instead of going after whoever's fault it was?*)

And then, the third time, was when he started collecting small-time debts for Marcella's creep—before the day she came home with the puffed mouth and the dark glasses. The cops must have given up on sweetness and understanding then and decided to try a little firmer persuasion, because that was when he got the work-over. So, naturally, he assumed he could expect more of the same this time. When it didn't happen, he decided the reason had to be they wanted something. The explanation came the next morning, in an interview room with a table and several tubular steel chairs, a recorder, and probably other monitoring devices, when Linc faced an interrogator named Breece from the DA's office.

"We didn't set all this up just to send somebody like you down. In fact, we're not especially interested in doing that. You could get off pretty light if you take a sensible line. We know you were working for a collector called Kyle Nass. In case you didn't know, Nass works for a man by the name of Carolton, who runs a line in casinos and loan hustlers. This angle that Carolton is playing has gotten a bunch of kids like you into trouble. That's what we're out to bust." Breece was a big, heavyset man with a full head of ginger hair, ragged ginger mustache, and eyes droopy like a bloodhound's. He shrugged in a way that seemed to say the rest shouldn't need spelling out, but the script required it. "This isn't the first job you've worked for them. You can give us dates, times, places that we can fit with other details we've got on record. Cooperate, and you could come out of it clean enough to get a real life."

Linc didn't try to disguise his contempt. "What do you take me for . . . even supposing I knew what you were talking about?"

Breece looked away wearily. "They're slime, Linc. You don't owe people like that anything. You didn't buy that line of theirs about juveniles being protected by special rights, did you? And if you do get nailed, they'll wheel in some big-time lawyer who'll take care of things? Yeah, right. Want me to give you the names of some of the kids they've flimflammed with that horseshit? I'll even let you talk to some of them if you like." Breece gestured impatiently. "Can't you see it's a scam? It's their way of keeping heat away from their own people—the ones they don't want to waste on the nickel-and-dime stuff."

The remark made Linc's cheeks burn. It was saying he was one of the unimportant ones, the expendables—not a professional. "I don't know any Kyle . . . whatever his name was," he insisted. "I just heard it around that this dude Colomada was in a hole for two grand and figured I could make a quick stack by standing in as the collector. Guys like that blab all over when they get under pressure. You hear it all the time."

Breece shook his head. "Not Colomada. He was planted, remember? One of ours. He didn't talk to anyone. You could only have gotten it from Kyle."

Linc shifted his eyes from side to side desperately, as if hoping an answer might appear on the walls. "It was somebody on the inside that I got talking to, who worked there on the accounts."

"Who? Give me a name," Breece challenged.

"I don't remember. . . . He didn't tell me."

"Okay, then. You tell me, what kind of account was it? Casino overdraft? Private note? Some kind of loan that Colomada took out with one of the sharks?" Breece waited. Linc had no answer. "It won't wash, Linc. You're going to take the bullet to protect scum. And they're going to walk—which is exactly what they set you up for. You get put in the freezer for the next five years, and they won't even be around. Do you think they're gonna bring you a cake on visiting day?"

Linc stared fixedly at the table. Breece was just trying to

put doubts in his head to get him confused. The thing to do was to tune out of all of it and not listen. *Be a professional,* he told himself, *and he'd be looked after. The Man—whether or not it was this Carolton that Breece had mentioned, Linc didn't know—always took good care of his friends. Kyle had said so.*

CHAPTER FIVE

SEVERAL days went by with Linc waiting to be told that a lawyer had appeared who would be handling his case, and in the meantime he had been bailed out. Instead, a woman visited him to announce she was his state-appointed defense and asked a list of insipid questions, making little attempt to disguise her distaste for him or the fact that what happened to him was not something that bothered her unduly. Linc told himself these things took time. Busy people couldn't be expected to drop everything and appear overnight just to put his mind at rest. He created mental pictures of events taking place behind the scenes—phone calls being made and papers filed, harassed prosecutor's clerks fighting a tangle of complaints and legal points. His father came to see him but had nothing useful to say. A social worker went through the usual dumb questions about life at home and what Linc did out of school. But as time passed and nothing more happened, Linc found himself getting anxious. Breece seemed to know it and stopped by for another talk at just the right moment to further undermine Linc's confidence.

"It's not looking good for you, Linc," Breece told him. "You were the mover who recruited the two jerks you were picked up with. Did you ever work with them before?" Linc didn't answer. "The one they call Clay already has a place in the book for carving up his brother's face with a carpet knife. Did you know about that? It happened over some dope money that went missing. The other one, Slam, has a mental age of twelve." Breece stared across the table, worrying at a tooth with his thumbnail while he gave Linc a few seconds to reflect. "A great pair to go down in flames for. You sure you don't want to change your line?"

Linc stared at his hands and said nothing.

"Well, I'd advise you to think hard about it," Breece said. "We might be going to trial against Nass and Carolton anyway, based on other evidence we have. But the case isn't as strong as it would be with your testimony added. In other words, you're in a position to make a decision that would please people who have a big say in how things might go for you from here. If there was ever a time to think about doing yourself a favor for once in your life, this is it. Do you get my drift, Linc?"

Linc would probably have held out doggedly come what might, refusing even to consider changing his story or compromising in any way, if it hadn't been for what happened a week after his arrest. He was taken by van to some offices adjoining the city court building, where he spent the next six hours sitting in waiting rooms in between seeing a series of people with the usual range of lines—nice guys trying to sound reasonable, through to table pounders shouting overt threats—all calculated to get him to change his mind. Linc wouldn't budge; through most of it he didn't even listen. Finally, late in the afternoon, Breece reappeared and received a summary of results from the last of the interviewers. In a muttered conversation outside the door, which Linc got the feeling he was meant to overhear, the interviewer told Breece, "Take him back. It's a waste of time. Nobody's going to get through to this one. He's gonna go down for max. Just dig a deep hole. You won't need a key."

A uniformed officer was detailed to take Linc down to the basement garage for transportation back to precinct headquarters, where he was still being detained. As they reached the second-floor landing, a sergeant in shirtsleeves appeared on the stairway above and called the officer back to query something on a clipboard he was holding. For a moment Linc was left alone by the stairwell, at the junction of two corridors of offices. Seconds later one of the nearby doors opened, and who should emerge but Kyle! With him was an almost bald, tight-faced man in a gray striped suit, carrying a black briefcase. Linc stared for a second, hardly able to believe his luck. He glanced up the stairs. The officer was still explaining something to the sergeant. Linc moved a pace forward into Kyle's path, causing him to slow. Linc gestured, expecting some sign of recognition. Kyle looked at him blankly.

Linc spoke hurriedly, in a low voice. "I've been trying to figure out some way of contacting you. Everywhere has to be bugged. I haven't told them anything. Is everything okay? When will I get to hear something?"

"Who in hell are you?" Kyle growled. Only then did Linc see the coldness in his eyes. For a moment he didn't comprehend but gestured again, making a quick shake with his head.

"Linc—Linc Marani. . . . Who do you think?"

"Never heard of ya."

"But—"

The man with the briefcase shouldered his way between them, his face mean. "You've made a mistake, punk. My client doesn't know you. You understand? Beat it." He took Kyle's elbow and steered him away. They disappeared quickly out of sight down the stairs.

"Marani, what's going on?" the escorting officer barked as he descended the half flight of stairs to where Linc was standing. "Stay right there. You don't talk to anyone, understand?"

It took Linc until the next day to face up fully to the meaning of it. He had been used. He had been set up. There was no intention to bail him out or help with his case. There never had been. Everything Breece had been trying to tell him was true. Kids like Linc were being sold a line and then dumped, while the hoods who made real money stayed clean. He found himself shaking with the anger building up inside like pressure percolating in a boiler as he realized how totally he had allowed himself to be had.

The obvious thing now was to turn his story around. He asked to see Breece again, and when Breece arrived Linc told him he'd decided to level. Everything was the way Breece had said. They wanted dates, places, details, names. Okay, they could take it all down, and he would sign. He didn't think too much about how he was going to handle the situation when he got out. All that mattered for now was to deliver as much as was within his ability to even the score.

And then, that same afternoon, he was told he had a visitor. It turned out to be a kid called Sammy, who went to the same school. Linc was mystified, because they had hardly spoken to each other, let alone mixed. Sammy's folks ran a sandwich shop on a nearby block, and he worked hard and stayed out of trouble. He talked vaguely about being sorry about the situation and hoped Linc wouldn't get hit too hard, and all the time Linc found himself growing more and more puzzled. And then Sammy said:

"I got a message to give you that your parents and sister are all well." He paused and frowned, as if working to recall words exactly as memorized. "Nothing's happened to them, you'll be pleased to hear. It will be nice if everything stays that way."

Numbness overcame Linc while a part of his mind tried not to accept what was obviously meant. Then it hit him like a cannonball in the stomach. "Who told you that?" he whispered.

"This guy who drove up on the street. . . . I never saw him before. But he was pretty insistent."

Breece came back later with forms, papers, a witness, and a stenographer. Linc could only tell him that the deal was off. He had nothing to say, and he'd take whatever came next. He wouldn't say why, and he wouldn't answer questions.

That was the first time that Linc had seen Breece lose his cool. He yelled and shouted, threw the papers in Linc's face, told him he was washing his hands of him and he hoped Linc rotted before he saw daylight again. Linc guessed he couldn't really blame him. In a way it was one of the rare times in his life when he'd felt bad for someone. But he'd make up for it one day, he vowed to himself as he was led away by guards to a van that would take him to a new location. They would pay.

Somehow, Kyle and Carolton would pay.

CHAPTER SIX

PROCEEDINGS against Kyle, Carolton, and whomever else the prosecutor might have had mind to rope in with them were dropped. Insufficient evidence was cited as the main factor, although frustration at Linc's last-minute change of position probably had much to do with it too. The consequence was that Linc carried the full brunt of all the resentments and bad feelings in the air. His defense counsel remained as lackadaisical, bordering on openly hostile, as she had been thoughout—to the point that Linc protested to Breece that any hearing based on a defense like that would be a joke. Breece nodded his agreement and laughed derisively. As a result, Linc ended up with a clear run of "Guilty as charged" on all counts. The sentence was detainment in a juvenile labor facility until age 18, at which time he would be transferred to the adult system. The term to be served there would be determined at that time.

Labor camp, Linc knew, was for the dregs, the no-hopes. It meant he had been written off as a lost cause. No remedial education, no rehab programs there. Just hot, aching, dawn-to-dusk grind, Marine boot-camp–style discipline, and rubber-hose educating or days in the cooler if he strayed an inch out of line. And afterward, when the review came up, they'd be pulling every trick in the book to keep him off the streets until he was being measured for a wooden suit.

But then, curiously, after pronouncing sentence, the judge informed the court he would be prepared to suspend it pending a decision on the availability of another option—and assuming Linc would be prepared to consider it. Linc was taken aback. They were giving him a choice? . . . It didn't take much thinking about, bearing in mind what he'd heard of the alternative. Sure, he told them. He'd be prepared to consider it.

Dr. Grober, Linc told himself as he was conducted into the interview office, was going to be a pushover. Two weeks had gone by since the court hearing. Linc had been moved to what was termed a transit facility, which consisted of five dormitory blocks and a communal building inside a wire fence, with desert outside and the scrub cleared back to a distance of three hundred feet. The inmates wore white shirts and gray pants, were kept busy for most of the day with things like clearing ditches and picking up trash from highways, but in between had access to a library with computers and books, and were permitted sports and workouts in the gym. So even if nothing came of the "alternative," agreeing to consider it put off starting at a labor camp by a few weeks.

On the day appointed for the interview, Linc was one of maybe half a dozen who were kept back from regular chores and assembled in a room in the main building, where they waited on uncomfortable chairs, avoided one another's eyes, and talked little. The procedure was sufficiently out of the ordinary to provoke anxious speculations, which long-formed habit caused them to keep to themselves. Eventually, Linc's turn came around, and he was called in to the room Grober was using.

Grober was perhaps in his late fifties or sixties, with white, crinkly hair and bushy eyebrows, a long, sharp nose, and mouth compressed into a downturn above a firm jaw. He wore black-framed spectacles, and his face was pink and florid, possibly due to the polka-dot bow tie he was wearing with a lightweight tan jacket. He actually rose from his chair when Linc was shown in. It was in a perfunctory kind of way that resulted from habit rather than anything given thought to, and he didn't go as far as to grace it with a smile. Nevertheless, that was when Linc decided that handling him was not going to be a problem.

Reformers came in two broad varieties, Linc had found. Mr. Strong-Clean-and-Honest offered himself as a role model. Usually opening with something like, "Well, a fine mess you've made of things so far, haven't you?" he played a stern, disapproving line—but with the suggestion you could straighten out provided you went with his rules. The fault was yours, but he could help you straighten yourself out. The right tactic in dealing with him was to accept the blame and then go for all the breaks you could get for as long as he went on believing his approach had produced a positive response.

Mr. Grieving-Understanding-and-Sympathetic, on the other hand, told you not to blame yourself because the fault was not yours but "society's," and with your help he could straighten things out. With him you played innocent and agreed you'd never had a chance—and then milked him for all the breaks for as long as he went on believing his approach had produced a positive response. All they differed on was the line they took as to whose fault it was—or went along with the appearance of taking, according to how they read the best chances of getting your cooperation.

Hence, Linc found himself unexpectedly flummoxed when Grober, after waving him into a chair, resuming his own, and allowing the guard to leave, stared at him in silence at some length with a curious frown on his face and said, finally, "You possess some interesting qualities, Mr. Marani. At least, based on what we know at this stage, we think so. It's true you don't seem to have put them to any especially useful ends, as of yet. But we're hoping that might be corrected. Would such a prospect be of interest to you, do you imagine: being useful? Needed by people?"

Linc didn't know what to make of it. He had never before encountered the suggestion he might be considered capable of being useful for anything. Being *needed* was an even stranger thought. He had always been told he was no good—even if in some cases, supposedly, it wasn't his fault.

"I'm . . . not sure I understand," he answered guardedly. "Where are you from? What kind of thing are we talking about?"

"Of course you don't," Grober agreed. "But it would be somewhat premature to go into that just now. The specifics can come later. For now I'm just interested in your reactions to a few points of principle."

He fell silent again, regarding Linc distantly, as if weighing up something in his mind. If this was supposed to be a sales pitch for some new rehabilitation program or to recruit subjects for testing another crazy psychological theory somebody had come up with, it was unlike any pitch Linc had met before. A few seconds more passed, and he got the feeling he was expected to say something. He jerked his head, his brow creasing in a frown, and gestured briefly. "You said something about 'qualities' . . . that maybe you might be interested in. I don't know what you mean. Just what are we talking about?"

"I'm not sure you'd understand if I tried to tell you," Grober replied. "Not right now, anyway. I said I wanted to put to you a few matters concerning principle. And you do have principles, you know, Mr. Marani. Strong principles—even if, at the present time, you are probably unaware of them as such. They are important things, you know. It's upon them that everything else is built."

None of this was making sense. Linc emitted a sigh of exasperation and shook his head, showing his empty palms. "Look, Mr. . . ."

"Grober. Dr. Grober, if you please."

"Maybe I'm being slow or something, but this isn't getting through. I can't tell you anything if I don't know what you're talking about. What, exactly, do you want?"

"Whatever you have and are willing to offer. I can't tell you exactly what. I doubt if at present you even know what it is yourself."

Linc put a hand to his brow and closed his eyes. "This is a game? Okay, let's try it another way. You don't know what you want, and I don't know what you're talking about. Then what are you offering? What am *I* supposed to think I stand to get out of it?"

"And there you have the game that marks our times," Grober observed. "Zero sum. What's in it for *me?* My gain can only be at someone else's loss. We build mistrust and antagonism into all our transactions and relationships." He made a face and waved a hand. "And the end product is the world you see around you. Everyone becomes a threat or a rival, an adversary to be squashed first before he does it to you, or the nice guy who talks you into letting down your guard because he's after your job. Violence and greed. Is history an inevitable product of human nature, do you think? Or do we unthinkingly and needlessly make ourselves prisoners of the past?"

Linc didn't follow everything Grober said, but the gist was becoming clearer. He shrugged. "It's how things are: Eat or get eaten. You go for whatever you can get, and hang on to what you've got. The corporations take you for what they can, and the government takes from everybody."

"Inevitably so, would you say?" Grober asked again. His tone was thoughtfully curious, as if the question had just occurred to him for the first time.

Linc snorted. "I don't know. . . . What is this? Do you think you're gonna change any of it?" Maybe this walking stiff did, Linc thought. *Okay,* he told himself, *he'd hitch along for the ride, just to see where it went. It couldn't be any worse than the camps.*

"I think this civilization of ours will be incapable of making further meaningful progress until it changes somehow," Grober said.

Linc eyed him dubiously, as if finally wondering about his sanity. "Is that something I'm supposed to care about?" he asked.

"Not in those terms," Grober conceded. "But the subject does have some relevance to the matter of what it is you stand to gain from the proposition I have to make. And that was your question, after all." He looked at Linc questioningly. Linc waited. "You ask what I have to offer. The answer is, nothing. Nothing, that is, for you to take. In fact, quite the converse." Linc's frown deepened. Grober went on, "What I'm offering is a rare opportunity—to learn how to give instead of take. A chance to discover service and obligation, and break free from the tyranny of expecting rights."

The words were so strangely different from the litany Linc was used to hearing every day that for a moment he had to stare hard to be sure he'd heard correctly. "The big deal is that I *give up* rights? That's what I'm supposed to go for in this?"

"Yes. Instead, to fulfill duty, know honor, and meet obligations. All of it priceless."

"Priceless? To be given obligations when I don't have any now? Is that what you're telling me?"

"Not to be given them. To accept them," Grober said.

Linc leaned back, shaking his head disbelievingly. "You really are crazy."

"At the time when such considerations become pertinent," Grober went on. "We would not demand unconditional agreement in advance."

And it was getting crazier. "Let's get this straight." Linc sat forward again. "You're saying I get to make choices in all this? It's not like some laid-down program I have to buy into up front?"

"Quite so," Grober replied. "I'll make no bones about it, Mr. Marani. What we're looking for is total commitment and obligation. The only truly binding loyalties are those entered into freely. This might possibly sound like a contradiction in terms to you at present, but that is likely to change with time. The only condition we would ask is that your parents or other legal guardians sign over their responsibilities for you fully to us for as long as we might deem it fit to continue."

This was unreal. Linc was finding it difficult to keep a serious face. "And right now I don't have to promise anything? I can go with it for as long as it suits me? You're happy to live with that?"

"It has been our experience that the best results are achieved that way," Grober affirmed.

Linc thought through what had been said but was unable to see where there might be a catch. Finally, he sighed, spreading his arms and turning up his hands in an attitude that said he had nothing to lose. "What else is there to say? If that's the way you want it, I'll buy. Okay, Mr. . . . Dr. Grober. I guess you've got yourself a deal."

CHAPTER SEVEN

CAMP Coulie stood at the end of a lake in a valley with boulder-strewn slopes rising to dry, rocky walls, somewhere in the mountain wilderness on the California side of the High Sierra. It had the feel of having been built originally as some kind of military base. Two rows of flat-roofed dormitory huts faced a block containing a messroom, a kitchen, and offices across an open square. Stores and a transportation depot flanked the square on one side, and a large hall that doubled as a gym, with various extensions and classrooms, was on the other. A fence surrounded the buildings but with an appearance of being intended more to keep intruders and undesirable wildlife out rather than the occupants in. Although superficially similar in some ways, it was an improvement on the state-run "transit facility," Linc decided.

He arrived there sixteen days after his interview with Dr. Grober, in a dusty, dun-colored bus that collected him from the municipal airport at Fresno, along with a dozen or so others who had arrived at intervals through the day, presumably from different places. They seemed to be around his age, the average tending to maybe a year or two older. It was a mixed group, perhaps half to three quarters of them boys. Two escorts rode with them in the rear of the bus, in addition to the driver and an armed guard up front. They wore light-tan pants and shirts—military-style but without rank indicators or insignia. Linc had been told to give only his first name or a nickname to anyone who asked and to say nothing about his background or where he was from. So, apparently, had the others. There was little talking during the two-hour drive, but a lot of surreptitious eyeing and weighing up of strangers thrown together, searching for hints of one another's measure. A black kid with curly hair had been at the transit facility in the same group Linc was in, that Grober had come to talk to. He recognized Linc, said his name was Rick, and made a couple of attempts at conversation from the seat opposite; then he fell quiet when it became clear Linc wasn't feeling talkative. In the seat in front of Linc, a huge, broad-shouldered youth with blond waves that reminded Linc of Kyle spread his elbows along the backrest, taking up the center and forcing the skinny Oriental next to him almost off the end. The skinny guy perched with increasing discomfort for a while, then moved to another seat. The climb into the mountains grew steeper, and the scenery more barren. Nothing had been said about the organization that ran the place they were going to or what its purpose was.

Others were already there ahead of them when they arrived at Camp Coulie. The dress for the inmates—or whatever term applied here—was evidently olive fatigue pants, worn either with a matching blouse or T-shirt. More tan uniforms were in evidence also, some of them with overvests in various bright colors. Linc couldn't really see them as guards, he concluded as took in the scene while the rest from the bus were emerging onto the dusty forecourt inside the gate. The people in the tan uniforms seemed more involved with what their charges were doing than *guarding* adequately described. *Supervising* was the word that suggested itself. It was quickly made clear to the newcomers that the term used was *wardens.*

After some paperwork formalities in the office, the arrivals were taken to one of the stores and issued three changes of basic clothing apiece, plus boots, two sweaters, a mountain parka and rainwear, along with blankets, towels, toilet items, and other sundries. Then they were assigned to sex-segregated dormitory huts.

Each hut had its own warden. Hut 3, where Linc found himself, was under the charge of a "Mr. Green." Mr. Green wore a bright green overvest. The bunks were two-tier, standing five along each side of the room. Some, including all the end ones, which occupied the corners, were already taken. Mr. Green told the newcomers to find a new home from the ones remaining—they would be here for six weeks, he informed them. Linc picked out a lower-level one with plenty of light near a window and moved toward it; but as he was about to deposit his armload of kit on the mattress, a folded blanket was thumped down sharply from the other side. He looked up and found himself staring at a pair of clear blue eyes set in a fleshy but hardened face, fixing him with a challenging expression. It was Blondie, who had sat in front of him in the bus. "Mine." The voice was little above a murmur, but menacing. The eyes asked the rest: *Any objection?* Linc held his gaze for several seconds, then glanced away. Although others were bustling about or seemed still undecided, Mr. Green had noticed and was watching from across the room. Linc locked with the blue eyes for a moment longer, then shrugged and turned to take the lower bunk adjacent instead. Rick, he saw, was already installing himself on the far side.

"The name's Arvin," Blondie's voice said behind him. "Better not forget that now, y'hear?" Linc ignored him.

Mr. Green assembled them around one of the bunks and demonstrated the required way to make beds and set out lockers. He then undid everything and made the owner of the bunk repeat it; next he went around with each of them until they could all do it right. A mini-lecture followed on basic rules and the schedule for the immediate future. There would be *no* fighting, "fraternizing" (for which everyone read "screwing around with the girls"), use of drugs or alcohol, or disclosure of personal history; theft of personal belongings, attempts at intimidation, or refusal of assigned duties would *not* be tolerated; there *would* be maintenance of self, dress, and quarters to the required standards, and observance of punctuality. The penalty for infringement would be "RPO," or Return to Place of Origin. In Linc's case, that would mean back on the labor-camp rap. It didn't take him long to decide this was good enough for him—he'd be sure to stay very clean.

For now, Mr. Green informed them, they could clean up and change after their journey. The showers were at the rear. If there were further immediate questions, he would be in his private quarters at the entrance end of the building. Dinner would be in the communal mess at 1830 hours. Tonight would be free time until lights-out at 2100. Tomorrow would start with PE on the square at 0600 sharp, after which the newcomers would continue through the day with cleaning and fixing chores around the camp while the rest of the intake were showing up. A general address would follow dinner tomorrow, by which time everyone should have arrived. Then they would all be able to get down to business.

CHAPTER EIGHT

AFTER breakfast, which spanned the spectrum from burned sausage to semiraw eggs, having been prepared by several of the inmates, Linc spent the rest of the morning filling potholes with gravel brought in wheelbarrow loads from pens in a yard behind the motor depot. Although he pushed weights and sparred to keep in shape, he wasn't used to this kind of work, and by lunchtime his arms and back ached, and his T-shirt was sodden from his exertions in the sun, which by then was high. Lunch was as big a disaster as breakfast, and there were angry exchanges between those returning hungry and thirsty from the heat outside and the catering shift who had been in the shade.

The afternoon was worse. Linc and a pudgy, pink-faced kid

who said his name was Royal—he was also in Hut 3, bunking somewhere on the far side—were detailed to take over the task of digging up a drainage pipe that had become silted, and cleaning out the trench for new pipe to be laid. The ground was hard and compacted, and had to be broken with a pick before any impression could be made with a shovel. A yellow marker indicated the target distance to be dug today.

There were less than a half hour into it when Royal complained, "I shouldn't be doing this. It's my back. I've always had a bad back." Linc paused from working the pick and looked up at him. The pink face was a plea for sympathy. He wanted Linc to go and say something for him. Linc grunted and went back to swinging the pick.

The clouds that had brought some respite in the morning had dispersed. His hands, sore enough then, were beginning to blister despite the gloves he was wearing. Royal straightened up, clutching a hand to his back. "I can't do this. I know I'm gonna hurt myself. You wouldn't feel bad at me if I tried to see if I could get switched to something different, would you?"

"Do whatever you think you have to do," Linc said tonelessly.

"I mean . . . I really have this problem. Ya gotta understand."

"Like I said, do what you have to."

Royal put down the shovel and walked back along the trench to where Mr. Blue—in a blue overvest—was showing a small group the technique of joining a new length of pipe. Linc watched Royal remonstrating and gesticulating, pointing back to where Linc had picked up the shovel and was beginning to clear the next stretch. Mr. Blue pointed toward the main block and said something Linc was unable to catch. Royal nodded and disappeared in that direction. Mr. Blue stared at Linc for a moment or two, and Linc thought he was about to assign someone else to replace Royal; but then Mr. Blue looked away and carried on with his lesson.

Linc worked on, getting hotter and itchier and feeling more put upon. Real smart, he told himself—he'd evaded labor camp for *this?* Some difference! For all he knew, this whole thing could be a scam. Maybe it *was* labor camp in the form of some stupid experiment dreamed up by another idiot psychologist. It was all he could do to prevent his anger from erupting into an uncontrollable display of rage when Mr. Blue looked at his watch, murmured something to his group, and sauntered away, leaving them to pick up their tools and disperse in a way that said plainly that their stint for today was over.

All except one.

He looked Mexican—dark and wiry, with a mat of cropped black hair and a grin that seemed to cut his face in half with a swath of white, even at that distance. He turned his head to gaze after the departing group, then back at Linc, gauging the distance to be dug to the marker. Then he strolled over. "Man, you got left with a bum deal here. You taking help applications?"

Linc leaned on the pick, pushed back the floppy brimmed hat he was wearing, and used the back of a hand to wipe his brow. The Mex had large, laughing brown eyes and a hairline of a mustache. "Sure, why not, if you're applying," Linc said.

He watched as the Mex took up the shovel and began clearing broken dirt from the trench. His movements were slow and even, and appeared effortless. The muscles flexed and rippled under his T-shirt. Linc went back to cutting the line toward the marker. Despite his forced effort, he was having to rest frequently for breath. The Mexican grinned at him without breaking his rhythm. "Not gringo's work, eh? You don't look to me like someone who is used to the sun. I give you a tip—soak the hat in water. The evaporation keeps you cool. A leather hat works even better. That's what they used to do, you know."

"Smart," Linc complimented. He tried to return a grin, but his lips felt cracked. "Wetbacks, I've heard of. But wetheads is a new one."

The Mexican's voice dropped to a more candid tone. "A guy is gonna need friends in a place like this," he said, revealing his motive. It was astute, realistic. He'd been around. Linc regarded him, sizing him up. The smile was direct and open, nothing crooked or sly, the eyes steady. Linc's gut feel was good.

He shifted the pick to his other hand and extended a gloved palm.

"Name's Linc."

"Angelo." The Mexican gripped and shook firmly. Linc winced.

"So, where did you do this kind of thing?" Linc asked.

Angelo made a face. "Some here, some there. Hey now, what's this? Are you trying to get me RPO'd on my second day here?"

"Forget it. You're right."

"Let's get this finished. Then maybe we'll have some time to lay back a little before we find out what the news is tonight."

The implication only hit Linc later when he was in the shower that, since there had been no one else around when they talked, Angelo had allowed for the possibility that Linc might be a plant. *I must be getting slow*, Linc told himself. Of course, with all the mystery and restrictions, there were likely to be planted ears in a place like this. Why hadn't something that would normally have been so obvious occurred to him? It had to be the traveling, the unaccustomed work, and the sun, he decided.

CHAPTER NINE

LINC and Angelo stayed together for the evening meal. Rick, the black kid who bunked next to Linc, joined them at the table, along with Kew, the Oriental that Blondie had pushed off the seat in the bus. Two girls, Karen and Shel, who had latched onto them, sat opposite. They were chatty but alert-eyed and watchful, on the lookout for opportunity and maybe—who knows, if the offer were right, the looks said—available. Linc remembered Mr. Green's warning and inwardly reaffirmed his vow to stay straight—at least until he had a better idea of what this was all about.

Dinner was actually not too bad: meatball stew with potatoes and crusty bread, followed by a fruit-tart dessert. Or maybe it was that everyone had worked up appetites so big they didn't care too much. Whatever the reason, Angelo insisted on going back to the serving counter with Linc to voice their compliments on the improvement. They buttonholed one of the makeshift cooks, a thin, dark-haired girl who had been scanning the room particularly anxiously, and Angelo told her what they thought. She stared at him and Linc for a moment, then burst into tears. It turned out the kitchen crew had been struggling all afternoon to try and get it right. She said it was the first thing she'd done in her life that had been appreciated.

After the dishes were cleared, the cooks joined the rest of the company in the hall. A rainbow of "Mr."s and "Ms."s in tan shirts and colored vests stood at the back and along the walls. "Mr. Black"—who by now, of course, needed no introduction—mounted the dais at the end opposite the main door. Evidently, he was in overall charge of whatever the operation was here. He was tall and leanly rugged, with tanned, heavily lined features and close-cropped hair showing gray at the sides. His face and chin were stubbly, either because he was starting to grow a beard or had been too busy to shave for a day or two. The talk around the room died and gave way to an air of curious expectancy. He began:

"I understand that everyone who was expected has now arrived. First, let me welcome you all to Camp Coulic, where you are invited to be guests for the next six weeks. Those of you who are still with us at the end of that time, and who wish to continue, will proceed to a second six-week phase that will take place at a different location. Details will be posted at a later date. In the meantime we've a lot of work to get through, and that includes more this evening, so I'll keep this brief. Apologies to those who've only just got here, but that's the way life is."

Mr. Black looked from side to side as he spoke, taking in the lines of attentive faces. He kept his manner neutral, seeking neither to win favor nor impress, speaking with a firm voice in a way that suggested somebody accustomed to carrying authority that didn't need to be flaunted. His hands, Linc noted, were large and sinewy, the kind that looked as if they could bend bars and split boards. That wasn't from scribbling notes and writing reports in a psychologist's office, Linc told himself.

Mr. Black continued, "This morning two people from Hut 4 were found inhaling crack dust. They were off the premises by lunchtime, and at this moment are on their way back to the places they came from. *Trangressions of the rules will not be tolerated.*" He then reiterated, one by one, all the rules that had been spelled out to Linc and the others shortly after their arrival. He then added a further point Mr. Green hadn't mentioned:

"I referred to you all a moment ago as *guests*. Let me make the meaning of that quite clear. Nobody is under any form of coercion to be here. Each and every one of you—and this will apply throughout your stay with us—can request RPO at any time, and it will be granted without question. However . . ." Mr. Black paused and glanced around again for emphasis, "for as long as you *choose* to remain, it will be on our terms. That's the only rule. The rest are conditions that you accept." He allowed a moment for them all to reflect on that.

"Waddya know. Guests," Karen muttered across the table. "I don't think I've ever been called a guest anywhere before." Shel snickered.

"Was your room all in order?" Kew said.

"Well . . . not bad, I guess."

"Considering the price," Angelo put in.

Mr. Black resumed, "Just to show that we're not all bad here, tonight you get to watch movies." A ripple of approving murmurs ran around, with one or two cheers. "But maybe these are movies that many of you have never had much of a chance to see." Mr. Black made a vague gesture in the air, which could have meant the room, the camp outside, or anywhere a hundred miles beyond. "Out there is some of the most rugged and challenging country to be found on this part of the planet. It can be beautiful; it can be lethal—just like a lot of things. How you fare with it depends a lot on you: what you're made of; how much you know. We're going to show you a little of the kinds of things to be found there, because in the next few weeks you're going to be finding out about them firsthand, yourselves. You'll also find out things about you. You'll find out what your strengths are and also your limits—where you need the help of others and what others have to rely on from you.

You'll know exhaustion and fear, maybe not a little pain—things that reveal people at their worst. But those same things can bring out the best in people too. You have a chance to discover parts of yourselves you never knew existed. We think they're there, otherwise you wouldn't be here. However, we're probably going to turn out to have been wrong some of the time. Make it your business to prove we weren't wrong about *you.*" Black showed both hands to indicate that he was through. "That's it. I said I'd be brief. Are there any questions?"

A lot of muttering followed, with quizzical looks being exchanged around the tables. Finally, on the far side of the room, a heavy, red-faced youth stuck up a hand.

Mr. Black acknowledged with a nod. "Stand, please, so we can all hear." The youth shuffled to his feet. "You are? . . ."

"Er, John. John Two."

"And? . . ."

John Two looked uncomfortable now that he had the room's attention. Somebody sitting beside him gave him a nudge. "Yeah, well, a couple of us here want to know . . ."

Mr. Black waited. "Yes?"

"Like, what it's all about. Don't we have some kind of right to know what's going on . . . you know? I mean, what's in it for us at the end of all this? Where are we supposed to be going?"

A few voices endorsed the question. Mr. Black, frowning, let them subside before answering. "Some kind of a *right?*" he repeated. "I think you still don't quite comprehend the situation. You are used to thinking of rights as if they exist automatically as things to be demanded and dispensed. But that was in a world that you are no longer a part of. We've all seen the trouble that belief has caused there. The only *right* that you have here is the one I've already indicated: to choose to return to where you came from at any time you wish. Rights beyond that, in the world that *we* are part of, are things to be earned. And they can be earned only by those who have learned to accept obligation. That's what you are here to learn. And strange as it may sound to most of you just at this moment, I can promise you that stands to be the single most valuable lesson any of you can learn in your entire lives."

CHAPTER TEN

FOR Linc, walking had always been a straightforward business of putting one foot in front of the other. It wasn't something that needed too much thinking about, and it did things like get you to the other end of the street. At Camp Coulie, he and the others learned there was a whole art to it. Walking over mountains, anyway. They learned it gradually and painfully in the course of the next two weeks, at the cost of blistered heels, swollen ankles, and muscles that could barely flex enough to get them out of bed the next morning. The even, strutting gait that was fine on city sidewalks didn't work here; feet hit rocks at the wrong angles or twisted and slipped into the cracks between. Each step had to be selected ahead by eye and measured, then made smoothly in a way that needed practice to flow into a rhythm that could be kept up for hours without the exhausting jerkiness and agonized gasping for breath that marked the early days. Learning to zigzag on the uphill slopes reduced the steepness; water took the steepest way down, so following creek beds was not a smart way to gain height. Legs could "freewheel" at almost a run on the downhill stretches, letting gravity do the work; better still, they could use the scree slopes of accumulated rock flakes from above as a makeshift ski run.

As the routines slowly became automatic, and toughened muscles allowed attention to shift from aching feet and pack straps cutting into tender shoulders, they began to see what was around them for the first time. One evening, when a group that included Linc was returning from an expedition to one of the local peaks, they came over a rise to be confronted by an unusually spectacular sunset even for the Sierra, flooding the valley with fire of gold from a sky writhing in violet and red. Everyone stopped and stared, transfixed. After a long silence, Mace, a hefty, red-haired youth, who hadn't said so because of the rules, but from his accent had to be from New York, breathed in an awed tone:

"Man . . . that's some hell of a fried egg."

Which at once broke the spell.

"So go write a poem to it or something," Flash taunted. Other voices joined in.

"Hey, give him a break, Flash. It's probably the most artistic thing Mace ever said."

"Yeah—so I'm feeling artistic today. You have a problem with that?"

"I got a problem with being half starved to death here. What did we do today—eighteen miles? Show me some real eggs."

Linc looked past them to Mr. Green, almost forgotten, taking it all in and watching. There was always one of the wardens there in the background—saying little when they weren't instructing, but always watching and listening.

• • •

It wasn't all just endless hiking. Aching limbs have to rest; raw feet need time to mend. Between the days of tramping along trails and over trackless mountain slopes, they painted fences around the camp, laid roofs, cut and replaced old timbers. They swam in the lake and learned to handle canoes and other small boats. They were shown first-aid methods and lifesaving. Everyone got to do kitchen duty too and found out what it was like to put up with the grumbling of hungry, worn-out cohorts back from the hills. The groan of "New kids in the kitchen" became a standard joke around the camp for any of life's tribulations that you can do nothing about and just have to put up with. Those who had already gained kitchen experience found themselves being sought out for advice. Everyone took a turn at hot, sweaty stints in the laundry.

On their rest days they got to try their hand at things like plumbing, electrical work, and vehicle maintenance. There were classroom sessions in recognizing plants and rocks, the stars in the night skies, and using map and compass. Those who were genuinely not up to sustained physical exertion were found jobs helping with the camp's day-to-day maintenance chores and in the workshops.

Linc preferred things that involved action and required physical coordination. He did well in the gym, found he had a good sense of balance and timing on the parallel bars, and after the first week or so could take the hikes comfortably. In the workshops he discovered a practical side to his nature that he never knew he had. Learning to use tools was surprisingly satisfying, and he found himself becoming fascinated by mechanisms. Class work, on the other hand, tended to bore him, and what little math he had absorbed at school wasn't adequate for the map-and-compass orienteering.

This was also a period of attrition. A quarrel that broke out in the kitchen turned into a knife fight, and both participants were RPO'd the next day. A girl from Hut 5 was RPO'd when the warden found her missing in a midnight spot-check. Royal, of the bad-back syndrome, pleaded sick two trekking mornings in a row and wasn't heard of again after the second time. Several more either couldn't or wouldn't fit and requested out.

At the same time, a growing air of competitiveness began making itself felt, which those in charge seemed happy to encourage. In fact, some of the more astute among the "guests" agreed it was the wardens who, in various subtle ways, had instigated it. Ratings began being posted each evening of the cleanest and best-kept huts, and the best times for athletic performances and hikes. Nothing was actually said officially, but spontaneous urges to better the other huts' scores began to emerge between the huts, and in some cases different groups within the huts.

Such gravitating together through a sense of shared pride stimulated social structuring around emerging leader figures. Mostly, this took place of its own accord, like the groupings in a school playground. Linc and Angelo became this kind of attracting binary (around which Rick, Kew, and several others fell into a loose cluster), with neither of them exhibiting any marked inclination to bid for supremacy.

In other cases attempts at asserting order were more imposed. A kid called Tommy from Hut 1, nice in his way but with a stubborn streak and quick to argue, was found badly beaten behind the gravel pen. He claimed he was jumped and didn't know who did it or why, and as far as anyone could tell, the matter was never solved. In Linc's hut, Flash, who took criticism badly and never accepted more in the way of chores than he could get away with, drifted into Arvin's ("Blondie's") orbit. The two of them stuck together, watching the others but not getting involved. Later, they were joined by a third, called Vic—clearly of Italian stock, with olive skin, slicked-back hair, a thin mouth, and narrow, mobile eyes that missed nothing. Linc quickly tagged him as a mean specimen to be careful of. All the same, the eye-blurring speed with which he could chop and dice with a kitchen knife astounded everyone.

The challenge came one evening, back in the hut after the meal, when Arvin was sponging mud off his parka. He indicated the can of water he was using and nodded toward Rick. "Hey, Rickafeller. Get me a clean refill in that from out back, willya?"

Rick looked up in surprise, hesitated, then stiffened in protest as he sensed the others noticing.

"Didn't you hear the man?" Flash asked after a few seconds. Rick faltered, then looked toward Linc in an appeal for guidance.

"What's it got to do with him? *I'm* asking you," Arvin said.

Linc found himself confused. Normally he would have seized the moment to settle right there the situation that had been developing for some days—he figured he could take Arvin. But violence was out this time, and he didn't know any other kind of solution. Unable to think through how to deal with it, he nodded a silent acquiescence. Rick picked up the can and, looking pained, headed for the washrooms at the back. Linc caught Angelo's eye and read concurrence that he had done the right thing. It wasn't worth it right now, over a can of water. But trouble was coming. It would be only a matter of time.

CHAPTER ELEVEN

HUT 3 had two Macs. One of them, inevitably, was dubbed Big Mac, upon which the other, logically enough, became Little Mac. Somebody transposed the latter into *Mackerel*, which thereupon stuck.

One midday near the end of the second week, a mixed group that included some of the girls from Hut 8 had stopped for a break on one of the hikes in a hollow beneath a broken cliff. The routes had grown longer, taking them higher into more rugged terrain. Campcraft had been added to the routine now, and on this trip they would be overnighting in tents and returning the next day.

"I'm telling you what it is; it's for the military." Beth took a swig of water and passed the canteen to one of her companions sitting and lying among the rocks. "What else do you think all this route marching and discipline is for? They figure if we're gonna cost tax dollars anyway, they might as well get something useful back."

"Makes sense to me," Big Mac said, gnawing on a chocolate bar and shrugging.

"A handy way to get rid of us as well," Mackerel added.

"Of increasing the odds anyway," Big Mac said.

"Well, gee, guys, thanks for making the day," a girl who was known as Cat said, making a face toward the others.

"Oh, Mackerel's always saying things like that," Angelo told her.

The wardens of both huts had come along to manage the combined group. They were sitting on a flat rock to one side, chewing sandwiches and sharing a flask of coffee. Mr. Green was studying the base wall of the cliff, which ascended perhaps sixty feet, in a series of slabs and fissures, to a ledge in front of a gully. The gully, choked with boulders and stones, led back down to the far side of a rocky mound jutting out from the cliff base. "Do you reckon you could manage to get up that?" he said to Ms. Blue.

Ms. Blue was blond, tanned, and lithe, perhaps in her mid-thirties, and began every day with a three-mile run. Also, she had gone through a high-diving routine at the lake one afternoon, which had suitably impressed the troops. She ran her eye up the face, from the foot of the wall to the ledge. "I think so. Does it need a line?"

Mr. Green shook his head. "Nah. Let's go take a look at it." They got up and strolled over to the base. Green stood for a minute or so looking up and surveying the choices. Then he moved forward, reached up to find handholds, and stepped up, wedging one foot into a crack and finding purchase with the other on a rock flake just above. Moving smoothly and maintaining a perfect coordination of tension with balance, he quickly reached the top of the crack about fifteen feet up and paused on a corner to plan the next stretch. The chatter below died as others noticed what was happening and began following with interest. Some stood up to watch. Mr. Green moved out onto a slab, climbed it deftly on tiny finger- and toeholds to an overhang—not large, but awkward-looking—where he had to try several different moves before pulling himself around it. From there he finished easily to the ledge, where he turned to sit straddle-legged on a rock at the top of the shelf in front of the gully.

"Not bad, Chief," one of the Hut 3 complement shouted up at him.

"Your turn," Mr. Green called down to Ms. Blue.

She followed the same route, obviously competent but taking it more cautiously. The overhang proved difficult, yet she managed it with the help of a hint or two offered by Mr. Green from above. Finally, she joined him at the ledge by the gully. Scattered but genuine applause went up from below.

"Okay, who's next?" Mackerel challenged, looking around. "We're not gonna let 'em get away with that, are we, guys?"

There was a short silence. Up above, Mr. Green and Ms. Blue had both disappeared from view and were coming back down the gully. Finally, a small but pugnacious kid called Todd, about Linc's age, stood up and crunched over to the base of the wall. "Sure, I can do that," he told the others.

Although he tried, he couldn't make the first foot jams in the crack to get started. Mace had a go, made it to about six feet, but then lost his footing, clung for a second, and had to jump, landing heavily with a yell and crashing onto a pile of dirt and rock debris.

"Are you okay?" Mr. Green asked, grinning as he appeared over the mound below the gully.

"Jeesh. I think I cut my knee." Mace inspected the damage. "My pants are torn pretty bad."

"You'll live."

Angelo moved past them to the starting point at the foot of the crack. "Here, let me have a try," he said.

"It's not as easy as it looks, Ange," Mace warned, wincing as he flexed his knee.

Ms. Blue arrived over the mound and joined Mr. Green. "Let one of us take a safety line up first," she suggested.

"I think I can handle it," Angelo said. Mr. Green shrugged

and nodded in a way that seemed to say, *Okay, if that's what you want to do. . . .*

Angelo started out splendidly up the crack to the point where Mr. Green had paused, and he too took some time there to consolidate. He began the move out onto the slab, and shouts of encouragement followed him. But then his movements slowed. Linc could see his fingers curling to find chinks to grip into, his head turning desperately, searching for a more secure stance.

"Don't hug the rock," Mr. Green called up at him. "Push out, and stand up straight on your feet. Balance with your hands—don't try to hang on them."

But Angelo had frozen. He was high enough now that a fall would be serious. Animal survival had taken control and wouldn't let him move from the position he was in.

"Keep him there," Mr. Green murmured to Ms. Blue, and went back to his pack to collect ropes and slings.

"Okay, Angelo, don't try to get any farther," Ms. Blue called up. "Stay right there. Relax, and keep your weight on your feet."

"*Relax, she says!*" floated down on the wind. Someone laughed nervously.

Mr. Green came back wearing a waist harness and carrying a lightweight nylon line with one end clipped to the harness. He also had a second line coiled around his neck. With Ms. Blue feeding the running line from below, he retraced his climb until he was alongside Angelo. He rigged a loop of line around Angelo's waist, then anchored a sling with a snap link a few feet above so the line ran up from Angelo, through the link, and back down to Ms. Blue. "Okay, Angelo, you can't fall," those below heard him say. "Now try and climb slowly back down. Ms. Blue will catch you if you slip."

But getting back down was a lot harder than getting up. Angelo came unstuck trying to regain the crack, and Ms. Blue had to lower him the rest of the way to the ground. By this time Mr. Green had repeated the climb and was back at the ledge by the gully. He straddled the edge again, secured himself to a sling passed around a knob of rock, and cast down one end of the extra line he had carried up with him.

"The lesson for today is: One, know your limits. Two, don't rush into things. And three, prepare adequately," he called down. "Okay, people, if you want to learn to climb we'll start again, but this time we're going to do it right. Ms. Blue will tie you on one at a time and go through the basics. I'll protect you from up here. Okay, let's get to it."

Most of them gave it a try. When Linc's turn came, he was one of the few so far who managed to make it past the first crack and onto the slab. As he continued to move outward, he became acutely conscious of his exposed position and the drop below, even though it couldn't have been more than twenty-five or thirty feet. Suddenly, he felt very precarious, as if any move at all would cause him to lose what fragile hold he had. Even though he knew the line was there to catch him, instinct overruled reason and made his body want to refuse to move. His hands were sweating and starting to slip on the rock. His feet began trembling under the protracted strain of balancing on his toes. Now he had an idea of how Angelo must have felt with no protection at all.

Ms. Blue's voice came from below. "You're doing fine, Linc. You have to make a long step with your left foot now. Go for it. You'll be okay if you come off."

Linc took a long breath, tensed, and made the move without really being conscious of it. Somehow, moving more automatically than by deliberation, he got to the top of the slab . . . but then came off at the overhang. Still, he was the first to have made it that far. Hoots of approval and slaps on the back greeted him as he arrived down at the bottom, bouncing down the rock on his feet as Mr. Green paid out the rope above. He found he was shaking as Ms. Blue untied him.

One of the girls also reached the top of the slab, and she made a spirited attempt at the overhang. However, her strength was gone, and she too had to return via the short way down. Her name was Julie. Although Linc had been aware of her presence in the group on the trek up, he hadn't gone out of his way to talk to her, although he had noticed she seemed popular with the other girls. Now he looked at her with a new curiosity. She was medium to tall in build, with black hair tied back and tucked inside her collar, and an attractive face tapering from high cheekbones to a narrow chin. Her eyes, a kind of icy blue-gray, returned his stare evenly as he stood watching her, his head cocked to one side, while Ms. Blue clipped the line to another of the girls waiting to take a turn.

"Not bad," Linc conceded finally, putting some effort into sounding as if he meant it. "Where did you do this before?"

"Nowhere. . . . I just couldn't let you get away with it completely."

Linc nodded slowly, all the time staring at her. "The overhang gets you. Whatever you try to do, you've got an elbow or something in the way."

"There has to be a way, I guess. They did it."

"I figure you have to straddle the corner wide, come right out of it."

"Let's see how Sal does." Julie looked away. "Okay, Sal? Yeah, right—that's the way I had to start. . . ." Linc watched along with the others, but he was more conscious of Julie a few feet away from him.

Sal didn't make it past the crack. Angelo had another try, this time with the rope, and reached the overhang; but he came off trying the same move that had defeated Linc. The only other one to get that far—to the openly expressed surprise of some—was Arvin. Huffing, grasping, pulling, he did it with no finesse or style at all—just brute strength, determination, and a total disregard for odds. At the top of the slab, he hurled himself around the overhang without even resting, as if even solid rock wouldn't dare oppose such a concentration of pent-up fury. But gravity refused to be repealed, and thirty seconds later he was back where he had started. A few voices gave him the credit that was due, and Flash helped get the harness off him. But Arvin's attention was all in the look he gave Linc. *Anything you can do, buddy*, the eyes said.

That, Linc saw then, was what the whole thing had been about. And just for a moment, when he looked at the fleshy features and the yellow waves of hair, he saw not Arvin looking at him so satisfied, but Kyle. All at once, the bitterness he had been suppressing through those weeks—or had simply been too busy or exhausted to think about—came flooding back in a rush. He turned back to Ms. Blue. "One more time," he said curtly. "Tie me on again."

It took Linc all his nerve and determination, back at the overhang, to force himself to do as he had said, and push himself out from the corner instead of hugging securely into it, and then to straddle the gap wide, feeling nothing below him but void. Yet it was the only way to reach the handhold vital for the next move. And this time he made it—all the way.

Mr. Green clapped him on the shoulder as he completed the final steps and hoisted himself onto the ledge to the accompaniment of cheers from below. "Did you ever do this before?" Mr. Green asked. Linc shook his head. "Then you're a natural. How would you like to try some more advanced stuff sometime?"

"Why not?" Breathless, Linc wiped his palms on his thighs and mopped the perspiration from his forehead. His hands were shaking, he realized. "There can't be much more of California left to walk over."

To one side of the throng below, Arvin, Flash, and Vic were not cheering.

The confrontation came that night, in front of the others, by the fire that had been lit for the evening meal. The two wardens had retired to Mr. Green's tent to check E-mail on the computer, get tomorrow's weather, and input the day's log.

"So how's the big hero?" Arvin sneered. Flash and Vic were flanking him a short distance behind. He thrust his face close to Linc's. "You might have fooled them, punk, but you didn't fool me."

"I don't know what you're talking about," Linc said.

"Oh, you know what I'm talking about. That little stunt up on the rocks today to make you look so good. You didn't do that on your own. We saw your friend Green giving the little bit of help with the rope—huh?" A hush had descended around them.

"If that's what you want to think . . ." Linc started to turn away, but Arvin caught him by the arm. Linc looked pointedly down at Arvin's hand yet held back.

"Who told you to leave? I didn't say you could leave." Arvin went on, "I say you set it up to try and make me look stupid."

Linc shook the hand away. "You manage that pretty good without me." Someone in the darkness guffawed. Arvin's face became ugly in the firelight.

"Okay, let's see how good you are without your friend around. Just you and me, out behind those rocks—right now." He jabbed a thumb, indicating several large boulders behind him. "Huh, punk?"

Linc sought frantically for a way out. He didn't want to get sent down over something like this, not after he'd come this far. But what kind of future would he be facing if he backed down? Arvin had the advantage in that at the moment he was driven by one single purpose, wasn't thinking, didn't care.

And then, without saying anything, one of the figures from the side stepped up alongside Linc to stand facing Arvin defiantly. Linc glanced at him. It was Angelo. A moment of stillness followed. Then Big Mac joined them on Linc's other side, followed by Mace, holding a brand taken from the fire. Mackerel, Kew, Rick, and others added themselves on either side, some also taking up sticks.

Behind Arvin, Flash, and Vic exchanged uncertain looks. This wasn't supposed to happen. "Ease off, Arv," Flash muttered. "I'm not about to get RPO'd over this."

Now Arvin's manner became less sure. He turned his head to look at Vic. Vic had raised a hand and was shaking his head. Suddenly, Arvin was on his own. He glowered back at Linc. Linc stared back expressionlessly. The others around him remained unmoving. Arvin could go for him now if he wanted—and maybe he'd get all of them sent down. However, the one certain thing was that if he tried it, the only way he'd be going back to his place of origin would be on a gurney.

"Okay," he growled. "So this time your luck's in. But don't think this is over." And he turned away and headed for the tents. Vic and Flash looked at each other, hesitated, and followed.

Linc stood, blinking dazedly. He'd won. *He* had been the one who was supposed to back down. Yet the solidarity the others showed had turned it around. And they had done it not because of something they stood to get out of it, or because they were bought or intimidated . . . but because of how they felt toward *him*. They had done it out of loyalty and respect for him. Never before in his life had he known a feeling like that.

Angelo was grinning in the firelight beside him. "Congratulations," he said. "I guess that makes you the boss around here now, doesn't it?"

Another figure had remained also while the others dispersed. It was Julie. Linc frowned, searching for something appropriate to say, then offered, "You didn't have to do that."

"I figured you'd earned it. It seems a few other people did too." She revealed the rock she'd been holding and tossed it down beside the fire.

"Well, I guess . . . Thanks." Linc had to work to get the word out. It wasn't one he had practice enough with for it to come easily.

"Well, just keep it in mind. Maybe I'll need a favor too one day," she said.

"You've got it."

Linc watched her as she moved away to join the other girls, heading for the tents. She turned and sent him back a wave with her fingers.

"Hmm. Quite something. I don't know that I'd want to risk getting RPO'd, though," Angelo commented.

Linc continued staring after her. "Don't worry, Ange. I've decided that whatever this thing is that we're on, I'm gonna see it through," he replied.

All the same, Julie was more fascinating than anyone he could remember meeting in a long time.

CHAPTER TWELVE

TO accommodate the social self-organization that was appearing within the camp's population, each hut was divided into two teams, designated simply *X Team* and *Y Team*. Heading and seconding the teams provided roles for emerging leaders and gave the others a structure in which to seek niches suited to their temperaments. As a general rule, the authorities tried to preserve the relationships that had come about spontaneously when naming the leaders, but they also intervened with judgments of their own where they saw fit. The original assignments of individuals to huts had been somewhat arbitrary, and the assigning of the two teams was used to move cases of obvious misfit and incompatibility to different locations. Every hut changed its bunking arrangements to separate out the X Team and Y Team along opposite walls. An additional dimension of rivalry within huts thus added itself to the rivalry among huts, although it tended to be of a more friendly sort. The other team, although obviously there to be bettered, was still "us"—an ally and a source of support in the greater enterprise—whereas other huts remained definitely "them."

In Hut 3, Linc became undisputed leader of the X Team and opted for Angelo as his second. But this was overruled, and Angelo was instead made the leader of the Y Team. This posed problems of divided loyalty among some of the hut's remaining occupants, who were given a first-preference option as to which team they wanted to be in. Linc had a suspicion this was deliberate—to confront them with having to make a difficult decision that couldn't be evaded. In the end, the majority, including Mace, Rick, and both Macs, came with him on team 3-X. Todd, and also Kew, unexpectedly, went with Angelo and 3-Y, which also received most of the transfers from other huts. Julie, to no one's amazement, was made leader of one of the Hut 8 teams, 8-Y.

Some had expected Arvin to disappear from the scene after the incident at the campfire. But as others pointed out, he had never actually *done* anything that the rules said warranted his removal. And as Mr. Green observed, staying at Coulie evidently meant a lot to him—people of Arvin's outlook didn't take lightly to losing face. He was moved out of Hut 3, however; and then, to the astonishment of practically everybody, it was learned he'd been appointed the 7-X Team leader. Hut 7 seemed to have collected most of the problem cases—the troublemakers who created discord wherever they were put, but never quite enough to get RPO'd. Unruly and continually squabbling among themselves, they were generally written off as far as chances in the team stakes went. But as time went by, and after a spate of bashed heads and discolored eyes that the wardens seemed disinclined to question, the Hut 7 teams began turning in some quite creditable performances. Perhaps Arvin's brand of talent had its usefulness after all.

Vic, who had the kitchen chopping-and-dicing skills, was

separated from Arvin and went to Hut 6. Flash, to the surprise of many, including Linc, stayed with Linc's team in Hut 3—after checking privately with Linc that there would be no objection. Flash was good with maps and figures, which was not one of Linc's strong points, and usually took care of the route planning and orienteering during expeditions. Reacting to Flash's obvious desire to mend bridges, Linc requested him as his second. Mr. Green promptly assented. Linc got the feeling that Mr. Green had been hoping for just that decision.

One evening some occupants of Hut 1 who thought they had clocked pretty good times for the running circuit and cross-lake swim posted their achievements on the general board in the mess hall with the caption *BEAT THAT!* Before the next morning was through, there was a posting that Hut 2 had done this, and by the end of the day every hut was taking stock of its repertoire of talents and proposing contests from log sawing to gymnastics that its leaders thought it had a chance to do best at. From then on, the sight of a noisy crowd jostling around the board to see who had set a new record for what, and what new challenges were being issued, became a regular feature of the evening. The hut wardens joined in too, and whether or not it was largely theatrical, showed every bit as much enthusiasm and commitment as their charges.

At the end of the third week—halfway through Phase One of whatever was going on—Mr. Black had the records posted of scores achieved in earlier courses at Camp Coulie. So now the huts were striving not only to be best among themselves but to be the best ever. Several of the team leaders came up with the idea of a tournament to be held near the end of the final week. The camp authorities agreed to it and didn't seem especially surprised; apparently that had also happened with the previous courses.

Of course, this quickly turned into a contest to see which hut would collect the most "golds." It was widely accepted that the first two places would go to Huts 2 and 6, which were exceptionally fortunate in their endowment of good performers.

Two blacks in Hut 2—inseparable from day one and instantly dubbing themselves "Amos 'n Andy"—were the best runners in the camp. There was a three-quarters Amerind called Patch—short for Apache—who seconded the 2-X Team and was in the same climbing league as Linc and only a handful of others. And just to gall everyone, the 2-Y Team, led by its hut warden, Mr. Brown, jogged—with packs—the last half mile home from a ten-mile hike, *singing* its way in through the gate to a version of the standard army chant:

We don't know but we've been told,
You guys 'round here are getting old.
Clear the way and watch Y-Two,
The best from Coulie is coming on through.

Hut 6, for its part, had three crack swimmers, a weight lifting buff, and the record holders for the mile in a two-man canoe.

In Hut 3, Mace was a strong swimmer, and Kew, lithe as a monkey, would score well in the gymnastics. The others included some good candidates for the team events. All in all, the hut leadership—Mr. Green, along with Linc and Angelo—figured that with the right choices they might have a fair chance for third place. This, while 2 and 6 vied between themselves to be first and runner-up, became the real prize the rest of the camp was shooting for.

CHAPTER THIRTEEN

THE chance that Mr. Green had promised Linc to try some more advanced climbing came a few days into the fourth week. Linc was one of a group of ten who went with Mr. Green and Mr. Orange for a day of intensive instruction on some crags at the far end of the lake. They learned to use ropes and slings, methods of tackling faces and fissures, the arts of belaying and rappelling.

The next day, Mr. Green and Mr. Orange took the same group up a long, grueling route that ended on a ridge three thousand feet up. Six of the most adept students, including Linc and Hut 2's Patch, were selected for an overnight expedition and introduction to snow and ice techniques that Mr. Green would be leading high in the Sierra.

They set out from the camp in one of the vans before sunup and began the actual climb from just below the snow line while it was still early morning. Through the day they labored upward across snow slopes and icefalls, pacing themselves slowly as they learned the new craft. By nightfall they were high on one of the ice fields not far below a rocky ridge, where they gratefully shed their packs, stretched aching limbs, and pitched camp. The plan was to cross the ridge and return to the van via a roundabout route the next day.

Linc had never realized there were so many stars or that they could be so brilliant. The air was cold. He sat in front of one of the four two-man tents erected on shelves cut into the ice, letting the heat from the mug of beef soup he was clasping warm his gloved hands. Nylon overtrousers and a *cagoule* worn on top of the layers of clothing muffling him and the *cagoule*'s hood pulled up over a wooden balaclava formed an outer skin against the wind. A loop of line clipped to his waist harness ran through a spike driven into the ice—an unprotected slip on the treacherous slope could send a person rocketing down for hundreds of feet. Above the level of the tents, peaks caught in the moonlight floated like ghostly icebergs on an ocean of night.

He knew now how to pick out the Great Bear, with its pointers to the Pole Star; the Belt of Orion; Sirius almost bright enough in the clear air to cast shadows. He realized as he watched that one of the points of light was moving. Some kind of high-flying aircraft, or maybe one of the bigger satellites. He'd never paid much attention to what people were doing up there: in the orbiting stations and space bases, on the Moon, and Mars, and places beyond. . . . (*Was* Jupiter farther away than Mars?) There were things in the news from time to time about something being built, or when an accident happened and people got killed somewhere, but he rarely remembered the details. They were like the billionaires who owned pieces of South America, or the war going on in China: things that just didn't figure into his life.

"Know much about what's out there, Linc?" Mr. Green

had been watching him as he sat a few feet away, heating water for coffee on a kerosene Primus stove. Water took longer to boil at this altitude because of the lower air pressure. That was another thing Linc had learned today—totally useless, but so what? It might win him a bet one day. He shrugged. "Like what?"

"Oh, numbers, for example. Do you know how fast light travels?" Linc shook his head. Although, there had been something once at school about it, numbers weren't his thing. "Fast enough to go more than six times around the world in a second," Mr. Green said. "One hundred, eighty-six thousand miles." It sounded fast, but since Linc had no concept of that kind of distance, he was unable to relate it to anything. "Yet the light from the Sun takes eight and a half minutes to get here; the light from the nearest star, over four *years;* and from some stars, millions of years," Mr. Green said. "Can you imagine how big that makes the universe? You could fit the whole world into the planet Jupiter something like fourteen hundred times. And Jupiter would go a thousand times into the Sun."

Patch looked up from the door of his tent, where he was using a knife to clean ice from his crampons. He was the only one still up with them, the others having turned in already. "So how long is a light-year? he asked.

"A light-year measures distance, not time," Mr. Green told him.

"Distance? A year? . . . How come?"

"Like you might say that Coulie is about two bus-hours from Fresno. Get it?"

"Oh. . . . Okay."

"Do you guys think you could get interested in things like that?" Mr. Green asked them. He made the question sound more than just idle curiosity somehow.

"I dunno. . . . I never really thought about it," Linc answered. He proceeded to do so—maybe for just two or three seconds; but they were the first ones in his life to be devoted to such consideration. "I guess, maybe . . . if there was some good reason."

Mr. Green nodded and seemed satisfied.

"This stuff's like concrete," Patch grumbled, grating the knife along a steel spike of the crampon he was working on.

Linc contemplated Mr. Green again while he sipped from the mug of soup. "So how about you?" he inquired finally. "How come you're into that kind of stuff? Have you been out there?" He waved a hand upward vaguely. "Is that something you used to do?"

"Careful, Linc. You wouldn't want to get one of the wardens RPO'd, would you?" Patch teased.

"Hell, nobody ever said anything about *them* not talking about where they came from," Linc replied.

"Mr. Green nodded. "It's okay. Linc's right." He looked away, up at the sky. He had a craggy face with hollowed cheeks and eyes that not only saw but interrogated everything. It was the kind of face that looked as if it had seen much and been through tough times. Although Mr. Green had never talked about much more than the matter at hand, Linc had formed an impression of him as quietly but forcefully competent in everything he did. He expected high standards but was always able to deliver at a level above anything he demanded from others.

Mr. Green looked back down at the billy, which was just coming up to a boil. "Yes, I've been out there. And one day I'll probably be going back. There's something about it like people used to say about the sea. You come back and say you're going to give it up, but somehow it always drags you back again."

"Some of us figured you had to be military—all of you guys," Patch commented.

"I've done some of that too," Mr. Green said.

"Is it true what some people think: that that's where we're all headed for, military recruiting?" Patch asked him.

Mr. Green snorted. "Come on, Patch, you know I can't answer that."

"What made you think they were military?" Linc asked Patch.

"Oh . . ." Patch waved the knife he was holding. "Who else would you wanna put in charge of some of the people we've got here? You could find yourself having to deal with some real problem situations, know what I mean?" He swiveled the knife to point it at Mr. Green. "Let's face it, man, we haven't given you guys too bad a time. It could have been a lot worse."

"True," Mr. Green agreed. "This course has gone smoother than some that we've run. We've had groups go on the lam, sit-ins with guests barricading themselves in huts. We didn't always do everything right. And probably we still don't. We're still learning too." After a second or two he added, "Don't you guys go getting any ideas, though. There's a PAT squad on call in Fresno that can be airborne in fifteen minutes."

Linc finished his soup and munched a biscuit, asking himself if any of the talk had brought him nearer to figuring out what this all meant. He decided it hadn't. As far as he could see, the military-recruits theory still made as much sense as anything. He looked at Mr. Green again, spooning coffee powder from a tin into three plastic cups by the light of a battery lamp, and thought about the places he must have been to that Linc had never heard of, the things he'd seen and done. In the same way as the things happening out among the stars, there was another universe Linc didn't know existed, ways of life that he couldn't imagine. There was a whole world out there, and he'd lived all his life on a few blocks of it—literally.

Was there more to it, where things worked the way they did at Coulie? Were there places where people were valued because of what they knew and what they could do, not on account of how much they'd been able to screw out of everyone else, or the wires their friends could pull; where others wanted to know you because of what you were, instead of what they thought they could get out of you?

Quietly competent, he thought to himself, watching Mr. Green again. Expecting things to be done right but always able to do better. That, Linc Marani resolved, was the way he wanted to be one day.

The next morning they resumed climbing. The weather was fine, and Mr. Green decided to carry on over the ridgeline above as planned. As they drew closer to the ridge, it resolved itself into a series of shattered rock steeples protruding through the upper snow slopes. The bleakness and total stillness of the surroundings were unlike anything Linc had ever known. There was a savage grandeur about it all that produced unfamiliar stirrings in him. Higher still but near now, the icy towers of the Sierra peaks stood outlined against the morning sky. To the rear and far below, the floor of California's Central Valley stretched away into haze, a miniature landscape painted on a carpet of yellow and brown and green. Down there was a world of invisible, scurrying people beset with their fears and their worries, working themselves into sickness or early graves, robbing and murdering one another over things that didn't matter. But to know the reality that existed up here, you had to look upward and climb out of that. It was the first time Linc had felt an inner conviction that he was capable of, and had been made for, better things. But exactly what kind of better things, or where he might find them, he still didn't know.

CHAPTER FOURTEEN

THE location for Phase Two would be a place called Seville Trace. All Linc knew about it was that it was situated somewhere near San Antonio, Texas.

It looked as if it had been built as a hotel and fallen victim to the wired interstates, which let drivers doze while vehicles cruised on robo-drive, with the result that people didn't stop as frequently as they used to anymore. Or maybe it had been undercut by the spate of unstaffed "motelmats," where machines took care of registration and dispensed all needs including disposable linen. Whatever the reason, it was now taken over by other interests for the continuation of whatever it was that had begun at Camp Coulie.

Linc and the others had thought that the purpose of the

operation might at last have been divulged with the completion of Phase One. They had expected something like a "passing out" parade, or at least a touch of ceremonials to honor those who had made it through, with maybe, as the culmination, an announcement of what it was all about. But nothing like that took place, and as far as that particular issue was concerned they remained in darkness.

They did hold the games at Coulie, two days before the end of the final week. Hut 2 just squeaked in ahead of Hut 6, and Hut 4 took the coveted third place. Hut 3, under Linc and Angelo, and Julie's Hut 8 tied for fourth place, and only two of the other huts managed to achieve golds. In Hut 7, Arvin personally took first for the bench press and runner-up for the squat lift. As with his performance at the climbing crag, it was done through brute force and determination. He'd never trained with iron systematically in a gym in his life.

But apart from that there was just a low-key winding down of everything, with another address by Mr. Black on the final evening, generally complimenting everyone and citing a few special commendations where called for. There were general rounds of farewells to the wardens—for whom, in many cases, respect and affection had become quite sincere and deep. But the overall tone was designed to restrain the inmates from getting too excited and carried away. The message seemed to be that whatever was going on wasn't over, and there was more to get through yet before letting up would be in order. They did all get a shoulder patch to wear, in the form of a doubled *C* motif set in gold against a red California sequoia.

About half those who completed Phase One at Coulie came to Seville Trace. The rest went to a different Phase Two, being held at another place. The remainder of the arrivals at Seville Trace were from Phase One staged at a place called Meyer Flat in Colorado.

Two two-story accommodation wings extended back from the ends of a front building containing offices, function rooms, and communal and dining facilities. The *U* formed between the wings contained a recreation area with a pool. Outbuildings erected on what had previously been the parking lot contained workshops, classrooms, and a gym. Standard dress was blue shirt and navy tie with a dark, tunic-style suit for the boys, ditto for girls but with a skirt.

Rooming was in fours, the slots being assigned, not chosen. Linc shared Room 207 with Patch and two of the contingent from Colorado—who wore blue shoulder badges showing a mountain peak. One with a Canadian accent, naturally enough dubbed Rocky; the other a black guy, Johnny, who sounded Jamaican. It seemed the general policy to mix the Coulie and Meyer people in this way. Flash, Mace, Rick, and Arvin were also among those who came from Coulie. Julie, however, was not. After their first brief encounter, intrigued by her as Linc was, the routine had been too demanding for him to get to know much more about her during the remainder of their stay at Coulie. The last he saw of her was as she was boarding a bus with a group leaving for Fresno a couple of hours before Linc himself was due to depart. He could have made a better effort, he told himself afterward.

Another face that Linc had hoped he would see more of, but who had presumably been routed elsewhere, was Angelo's. Both of Hut 3's "Macs" were missing from Seville Trace too.

The staff wore the same style of tan uniforms as had those at Coulie. Phase Two would focus on assessing schooling and identifying proclivities for technical, artistic, or other skills, and the names that most of the staff went by reflected the various specialty subjects they covered, such as Mr. Hacker, Ms. Writer, Mr. Math. The objective, the new intakes were told by the Director in an introductory talk reminiscent of Mr. Black's at Coulie, was not to shoehorn them into categories or any particular role but simply to uncover and get a measure of aptitudes. Everyone had their usefulness. The unusual, the oddball, the rare talents, were of special interest. They were what Phase Two was aimed at singling out.

Room 207 was on the outside of the block, facing the highway about a quarter mile away, where the drone of robo-trucks passing at precise one-minute intervals continued through the night. The room was doubtless more functional now than when the establishment had been a hotel, containing two single beds on either side of a central table, with chairs, a double bureau, shelf units, a shared hanging closet, and individual lockers for other clothes and personal effects. On the day following their arrival, Linc and his three roommates were resting up in the hour and a half of free time after the evening meal. It had been a day devoted mainly to becoming familiar with the program and organizing schedules. The Phase One program at Meyer sounded as if it had been similar to that at Coulie, ending also with a spontaneously organized contest of games. As was often the way when there was nothing pressing to attend to, the talk drifted around to what the purpose of the operation might be. Nobody was any nearer an answer, but they never tired of speculating on the subject. By now, few of the speculations were new.

"Most of us at Meyer figured it has to be free meat for the army," Rocky said, lying stretched out along his bed by the window, his hands clasped behind his head. He was long and gangly, though with strong arms like cables of knotted gristle, and had an angry, jagged scar across one cheek.

"Yeah, that went around Coulie all the time too," Linc said. His tone conveyed that he didn't subscribe to the view, especially.

"What else could it be?" Rocky asked.

Linc shrugged. "I'm not saying it isn't. I'm just saying that no amount of guessing is gonna change anything. We'll know when they tell us."

"I still think it could be somebody's idea of some new kind of rehab scheme," Patch said from the table, where he was whittling a horse head from a piece of oak. Patch always had to be doing something. If he wasn't deicing crampons, cleaning his shoes, or sewing something that needed mending, he carved things from bits of wood. The others said it was because he had totem poles in his genes. His mention of rehabilitation was an acknowledgment of what just about everyone had tacitly recognized: that by their general speech and manner, and the subtle, unconsciously registered signs that each kind has of knowing its own, the inmate population was made up of elements from that side of society that would be referred to in polite company as socially deviant. It was about as close as anyone came to talking about individual backgrounds, which was still on the prohibited list.

Johnny was relaxed and easygoing, with skin as black as any that Linc had seen. His huge white grin had earned him the nickname Piano Man among the Meyer people. It was surely no coincidence that all four of them put together in Room 207 were former Phase One team leaders or seconds.

"Why all this thing about the army and the military all the time?" he asked the others. "There's plenty other outfits out there that'd pay good money for extra help that they didn't have to go payin' no taxes an' insurances on, an' all that stuff. An' 'specially if they can be pretty sure you ain't gonna go walkin' nowhere." Johnny had a soft, lilting way of speaking that Linc found easy to listen to. At the same time, he got the feeling that with little effort Johnny's voice could become very menacing.

"Sounds to me that what you're talking about now could be getting close to what you might call slave labor," Patch said after reflecting.

Johnny laughed delightedly. "You think that's somethin' new with those people? What else would you call them givin' you a gun and tellin' you they gonna lock you up 'less you go kill people you never heard of to make the world safer for money that you ain't got? An' what about all them guys out there workin' two jobs, all rippin' each other off for the corporations jus' like the other guys who are shootin' each other for the governments? What's the difference? The only crime we got picked out for was workin' for ourselves instead o' handin' it all over. Far as I recall, at one time that was what used to be called bein' free."

"Watch it, Johnny," Linc cautioned. "Don't start getting carried away with histories now."

"Oh, yeah, right. . . . I still say, though, that what they call criminal is just about the only honest way to make a livin' that there is left."

Rocky raised his head to look across at them. "Johnny's got

a point, though. All of this hiking around mountains and running courses to see how you shape up doesn't have to be for the military. Maybe the scam is to find people the corporations can send to work in places where the regular labor price would be sky-high."

"Especially if the wastage rate gave you poor numbers for the return on the investment," Johnny pointed out, smiling nevertheless.

"Now tell me that isn't slave labor," Patch said.

"What kind of places, for instance?" Linc asked Rocky.

Rocky lay back to contemplate the ceiling again. "Oh, I don't know. Some of the deserts, or the mining you hear about out in Siberia, maybe. Then there's the deep-ocean extraction rigs. It could be even the stuff they're always talking about setting up to do on the Moon. That is right, isn't it? Aren't there supposed to be new things going on up there?"

Linc thought back to the night when he and Patch had sat with Mr. Green, high in the clearness amid the Sierra Nevada peaks, and stared out at the stars. "Or maybe even farther away than that," he said distantly.

CHAPTER FIFTEEN

THERE were no teams or leaders at Seville Trace to encourage performance by stimulating competition. That arrangement had now served its purpose of awakening self-esteem and bringing some functional cohesion to an initially totally disparate intake of individuals of all types and backgrounds, and it was properly left behind with Phase One. The rooms were not asked to designate a spokesperson or senior member, and neither was one appointed. However, each floor had assigned to it two full-time staff members known as coaches. With an upper and lower floor in each of the two wings, twelve rooms to a floor, this meant there were eight coaches. Four of them took names after the seasons of the year, and the others after the four playing-card suits. Their job was to work individually with the people in the six rooms under their charge, helping them to plan a work schedule that was right for them and to assess their progress.

The coach for Rooms 207 to 212 was Mr. Summer. Remedial tuition was available for those needing to catch up on basics, and one of the first things he felt necessary in Linc's case was to put him in one of the math groups. Linc's restlessness with classroom subjects was apparent in his report from Coulie, and to balance things they worked out a schedule that included time in the basic metalworking and machine shops.

Linc found himself taking to it almost as naturally as he had to climbing. Shaping, cutting, and finishing a piece of metal to perform a precisely designed function intrigued him. All his life he had been surrounded by things formed and crafted out of what had started as raw rock, from the cutlery he ate with and the watch bracelet on his wrist to the parts making up the satellite he had watched crossing the night sky over the Sierra. Yet never once had it crossed his mind to wonder where these things came from or how they were made and put together. The few workshop sessions he had taken at Coulie had provided a first glimpse into the subject, and it interested him. Mr. Summer thought it would be a good idea to let that discovery develop further. It didn't follow, necessarily, that Linc's calling in life was to be a tool-and-die fitter or instrument maker—precision skills that took years to acquire; but the experience could be a first step to opening up large areas of applied science and engineering to be explored more fully, should it turn out that Linc had talent in that direction.

In addition to these things, there was still Linc's penchant for physical action and the need he had demonstrated for pitting himself against exacting challenges. To take this into account, Mr. Summer recommended the martial arts class being run by two black belts, a Mr. Throw and Ms. Punch. Linc assented readily—thinking inwardly, though he didn't say so, that he might even have a few tricks of his own to contribute. As had proved true of climbing and of working creatively with his hands, he found that martial arts were something he took to instinctively.

And that was where he next ran into Arvin.

"Okay, people, that was good," Mr. Throw called to the class of a dozen paired off around the mat. The agenda so far had been the basics of judo. "Everybody change opponents, and we'll have free sparring for the rest of the time."

Linc separated from Hash, with whom for the past fifteen minutes he had been taking turns going through the movements of a sweeping hip throw—in which the thrower pivots to make the throw over his back on one leg, using the other to sweep the opponent's legs away in a backward reaping motion. They made the customary quick bow from the waist, and before Linc had a chance to look around for a different partner, Arvin came over and seized the lapel and sleeve of his *judogi* in the normal stance to begin combat. Although not the first class for either of them, this was the first they had attended together. Until now, Linc had tried to ignore Arvin's presence and stay out of his way. As far as Linc was concerned, the earlier business between them was over.

They moved around the mat, sizing up each other's style and watching for openings. Normal practice was to keep the hold on one's opponent light, using touch as a sensory device to read his movements and avoid the telegraphing of one's own intentions that too rigid a grasp would entail. But Arvin twisted his fists solidly into the material of Linc's jacket and proceeded to direct their course around the mat, first advancing while delivering a series of provocative shoves, then falling back and tugging, causing the collar to saw painfully against Linc's neck. Linc felt like a rat being shaken by a dog. He tried turning and closing to attack as they had been shown, but Arvin's arms held him off like iron bars. All the time, Arvin was hacking at Linc's shins and ankles first with one foot, then the other. Properly timed, an ankle throw delivered with the sole caught an opponent's foot just as it left the floor or was about to make contact with it, and could sweep the opponent's feet up over his head. However, Arvin was kicking out at Linc's feet when they had weight on them and were pinned. He wanted to hurt, not throw.

Then Arvin turned and came in low to try a shoulder throw; but it was mistimed, and Linc evaded it. Arvin tried two more moves, using his strength to pull Linc into him rather than letting Linc's own movements draw him on. Linc could only break away by meeting force with force, which was inelegant and not in keeping with what they were supposed to be learning—but he stayed on his feet. Then, abandoning all pretense of abiding by the spirit of things, Arvin practically lifted Linc off the ground with his hands and heaved him over a hip, straightening his arms as Linc went down to propel him harder at the floor. The impact was too fast for Linc to fully apply the break-fall technique that they had been shown, and his breath was knocked out of him as he thudded into the mat.

"Ease up over there, Arvin," Mr. Throw's voice barked from across the floor.

"Yes, sir," Arvin acknowledged. Yet he was smirking as Linc picked himself up. "Not so great without your buddies around, eh?" he muttered as they closed and took their holds once again.

They circled, feinting and lunging. Arvin tried the same move twice again, but Linc was ready now and both times pulled himself clear. Then Arvin opened up and took a long step in for a trip, offering the ideal lead into the throw that Linc had just been practicing. Moving instinctively more than under conscious direction—the way he had when he climbed the slab—Linc spun inside the arc of Arvin's chest and shoulder, using his momentum to carry both of them together into the turn. Everything connected perfectly. Linc's sweeping leg took Arvin off the ground to wind him around Linc's arched back, catapulting him on and over with barely a sensation of any weight at all touching Linc's body. Arvin crashed heavily, and Linc heard the distinct *crack* of his teeth coming together.

"Good point, Linc!" Mr. Throw called over. "Don't forget to breakfall, Arvin. Strike down hard. Use that arm."

It had been mostly a fluke, but Linc didn't let that spoil anything. Arvin was still gasping when he stood up. His face was mean as he grabbed again for Linc's jacket—both lapels this time. Just for a moment, Linc didn't register the altered grip. Mr. Throw turned away to demonstrate something to another of the pairs; another pair moved in between. . . . And suddenly all Linc knew was a flash of colors and *pain* blotting out everything else.

The next he was conscious of was that figures were gathered around him. He was still standing, aware in a detached kind of way of blood pouring down over his jacket, Arvin in the background, his hands raised high, proclaiming innocence. "An accident. . . . Sorry, guy."

Mr. Throw was peering at Linc, tweaking his nose. Another surge of pain. "Well, it doesn't seem to be broken, at least."

They took him to the showers and swabbed him with a wet towel while others disappeared back out with a bucket to sponge the blood off the mat. Mr. Throw put a call out for Ms. Medic, who arrived shortly after and taped a dressing across Linc's nose when the bleeding had stopped. By the time Linc had cleaned up and dressed, the rest of the class had been dismissed.

"Feeling okay?" Mr. Throw asked as he bundled the bloodstained towels and clothing into the laundry bin.

"Oh . . . still kind of dizzy. A little bit sick."

"That's to be expected." Mr. Throw studied him silently for a few seconds. "Want to tell me about it?" he invited.

"What's there to tell? We bumped heads. It was an accident."

Mr. Throw shook his head. "That wasn't any accident. I saw the way you two were going at it before it happened. You're both from Coulie, right? Is it to do with something that happened there?"

Linc looked away, his face betraying nothing. "It's okay. It'll take care of itself," he said.

Mr. Throw gave him a moment or two longer to consider,

then nodded. "Just don't go doing anything to get yourself RPO'd over," he said. "It's not worth it."

Flash stopped by later that afternoon, when Linc was in the machine shop. He had been put in Room 105, which was on the floor below Linc in the same block, and was taking a lot of classes involving computers. He had fair curly hair and a big nose, and his general manner had brightened since the early days at Coulie. He and Linc had worked well together as things turned out, and Linc was happy he had made a good decision back at Coulie in choosing Flash as his second.

"I heard you'd collected a mask," Flash said, sauntering up to the lathe at which Linc was working. "What happened?"

"I bumped into our friend again—literally."

"Arvin?"

"Uh-huh."

"Uh-oh." Flash shook his head. "How?" Linc told him the story while he worked on. "That's bad news," Flash said when Linc was through. "If he's got it in for you, he won't quit."

"Even if it gets him thrown out?" Linc found it impossible to believe. "Didn't Green back at Coulie say that staying in was important to him? You think he'd risk it?"

"No," Flash said, shaking his head. "He'd find another way."

After Flash had left, Linc made the last, fine-finishing cut on the piece he had been turning, then parted it from the metal stock that it had been cut from in the lathe chuck, and examined it. He felt a strange wonder at the thought of making something like this with his own hands. In a way it was like creating a sculpture—releasing the shape that had been imprisoned in the metal. The luster and smoothness of the gleaming piece intrigued him. He began to understand the compulsion that throughout history had driven some men to crave the possession of gold.

His gaze traveled over the precisely fitted parts of the vernier, micrometer, and other tools he had been using; at the lathe itself, with its lead screws, tool turrets, and gear trains.

One day he wanted to be an artist who could create such forms out of metal, forms exact enough to come to life when they worked together. On their own, as separate parts, they could do nothing. But fitted together in the right way, each contributing its own particular function, they could do anything.

It was very much the same, he thought to himself, *with people*.

CHAPTER SIXTEEN

VIC was one of those who had been routed elsewhere at the end of Phase One. With Flash's transfer of allegiance to Linc, this had left Arvin pretty much on his own for a while after moving from Coulie. But then he found himself a new sidekick who called himself Welsh, a Southerner, maybe from Alabama or Georgia from his voice, with a mean-eyed face formed of ruddy crags that made him look twice his years. Welsh worked part of the time as the machine-shop and workshop storekeeper, responsible for issuing tools and materials. It was uncanny how, after Arvin and Welsh got to be friends, mix-ups always seemed to occur when Linc was involved, but never with anyone else.

"Hey, Welsh." Linc showed him a broken tool bit. "This is

the wrong one for the alloy I'm working on. It chewed right up."

"Hell, lookit that. Someone musta turned it back in the wrong box."

"It's ruined the piece I was making."

"Isn't life just a bitch sometimes."

On another occasion, when Linc started up a pillar drill after coming back from the rest room, a steel chuck key that had been left in the chuck—on the far side from him, where he couldn't see it—flew out like a bullet, narrowly missing a girl working at a milling machine twenty feet away. Mr. Turner, who was in charge of the shop, was not amused.

"That could have killed somebody," he said. "You ought to know better, Linc. That was one of the first things you learned here."

Linc *never* left a chuck key in, even for a few seconds. But arguing would only have made things worse.

He was bumped by people passing in the corridors, shoved when standing in line in the cafeteria. The clothes in the bag that came back from the laundry were three sizes too small. "The wrong tag musta got put on," he was told when he took them back. "Dunno how that coulda happened. . . . Nope, sorry. No sign here of yours at all."

He had no doubt that Arvin was behind it. It was as if Arvin took it that the incident in the gym finally settled that he had come out on top, and Linc couldn't be allowed to forget the fact. Linc tried to put it out of his mind and concentrate on the different way of seeing life that he was beginning to discover.

It took hours of patient work to create something as intricate as a precision instrument, years to acquire the skills to do it; and what made it possible beyond that was knowledge that had been built up over centuries. Yet any jerk with a hammer could destroy it in seconds. Since there were so many jerks loose in the world, it seemed that nothing complicated or demanding should ever get made. Yet the machines that he worked with were here; every day, planes climbed skyward from the San Antonio airport, a few miles away. When they put their minds to it, people could create so much more than they destroyed.

Something in their nature seemed to drive them that way. Linc would have liked to see a world in which more of that could happen. He wanted, somehow, to help make it happen.

It was after seven in the evening. Swimming and diving classes were over for the day, and the pool was free for recreation. Linc and Patch hung in the water with their arms draped along the edge, enjoying the coolness after a hard day. Johnny was on cleanup duty in the front building. Rocky had asked them to stay away from the room for an hour, and they hadn't asked why. He had been keeping company with a girl called Liz, from Room One Hundred–Something on the ground floor of the other wing.

"I hope we're still together when we get wherever this is heading, and it's okay to talk about ourselves," Patch said. "I've got a story for you that'd keep us up all night. There's something that tells me yours wouldn't be all that uninteresting either."

"If you're fishing, Patch, forget it," Linc told him. "When it happens, I plan on still being around."

"Still playing it straight and even, eh, Linc? Not taking any chances. Not like Rocky."

"He's crazy. They know everything that goes on in this place—it's like in the slam. It could even be bugged everywhere for all we know."

Patch made a face. "Aw, I dunno. This just doesn't strike me as that kind of an outfit somehow."

"How could you tell?"

They turned their faces away as somebody jumped in off the side, making a large splash nearby. Patch wiped an eye with the back of a hand. "Do you still reckon it could be something in space like you said—corporations? I asked around about it. A lot of guys think that could be right."

Linc shrugged. "Like I said before, you can guess all you want, but it isn't going to change anything. Why waste the time?" He looked away. On the far side of the pool, a girl called Marlene looked as if she had spotted them and was coming around. He added, "But if it's right, and we are still together, I don't know if we'd be able to get in much climbing out there."

"Not on the Moon?" Patch said. "Doesn't the Moon have mountains?"

"More like just dust everywhere from the pictures I've seen."

"I thought it had mountains. Isn't all that white stuff you see ice? . . . I've seen pictures on TV of bases and tractors and things, with all this ice everywhere."

"That's not the Moon we see. It's other moons someplace else," Linc said.

"Really?"

"I think so. . . . But it's something we can still do when we get time off," Linc said. "Whatever this thing is that we're into, we're bound to get leave or vacations or whatever sometime. When that happens, we'll get our own stuff together, and we'll go to the mountains ourselves, somewhere. And we'll climb."

"Hey, you really mean that? It sounds great! You're on, man! We'll do that. It's a deal." Patch grinned and held up a hand. Linc slapped his own palm into it.

"Deal!"

"Hi, guys. Cooling off?" Marlene lowered herself to sit on the edge by them. The pool area was starting to get crowded as more people came out to make the best of the free time.

"After a day like this one, I could use it," Linc said.

Patch stretched out to let himself float, still grasping the rail with his hands. "Just hanging in here."

"Seen Rocky about?" Marlene asked, looking around. She managed to sound *too* casual about it. Linc got the feeling that she was more curious about who Rocky was supposed to be with.

"Not lately," he replied.

"I think he might be working," Patch said.

"Oh." The air of chatty intimacy switched itself off. "So, what did you guys do today?"

Linc made a face, rocking his head from side to side. "Oh, workshop stuff that you probably wouldn't want to hear about.

An hour in the gym. Floor-scrubbing detail in the kitchen. All kinds of wild things."

"I saw you in the library at lunchtime," Marlene said.

"That's Linc's new room," Patch told her. "We're gonna put a pool table in the space where his bed is. He doesn't need it."

"What's so interesting in the library?" Marlene asked.

"Math and trigonometry," Patch said. "Would you believe he sits in there and reads math?"

"The final machine-engineering practical tests are in a few days," Linc explained. "You have to make a set of test parts to drawings, and they get graded. The dimensions that aren't given have to be calculated."

"It sounds really like my idea of fun," Marlene commented.

"It's what he wants to do," Patch said. He braced his arms against the side of the pool and lowered his legs until his feet were pressing against the side as well. "And what I want to do is stretch a little and get some lengths in before this gets to be wall-to-wall people. That's what I came here for. . . ." So saying, he pushed away, turned to head in the lengthwise direction along the pool, and broke into an easygoing crawl.

"So what're you aiming for?" Marlene asked, looking back at Linc after a few seconds. "Some kind of engineer or something?"

"I don't know yet. Maybe something like that, yes."

"You seem to take it seriously," Marlene said.

Linc nodded distantly, his eyes on the far side of the pool. "Maybe there's a time when people need to start doing that."

"Your nose is looking better anyhow."

Linc turned his head and looked up. She was watching him curiously, her head tilted to one side. He no longer needed the dressing, and the flesh was almost back to its normal color. "You figure my looks will keep then, huh?" He grinned.

"Oh, your looks are pretty okay anyhow, never mind the nose." Marlene seemed to think for a moment, as if the line had given her a cue that she wanted, then looked back, seemingly weighing him up. She glanced around, and her voice fell. "You know, sometimes everyone needs a break from all this thinking. If you wanted to, kind of . . ." She let the suggestiveness in her voice say the rest for her. "I know a place."

Linc leaned his head back against the side of the pool and closed his eyes. "A nice thought, but . . ." He shook his head. "I plan on being around when this thing gets wherever it's going. I guess it's gotten me curious now."

"Huh. Maybe I need to be put together with nuts and bolts or something. Who do you get off on, Frankenstein's daughter?"

Linc grinned. "You're put together just fine, Marlene. But I don't want to blow this chance now. It's different from all the other things I've known. I want to know where it goes."

There was a sigh. He heard her straightening up. "Okay. I just wish I could see something like that in it. . . . I'll see you around."

"Sure thing."

"Oh." Marlene's voice came from slightly farther off. "And good luck with the tests."

"Thanks."

Linc relaxed in the water for a moment, then opened his eyes and turned to rest his elbows on the edge and watch her as she walked away. Not bad looking, in a zesty, sporty kind of way, he had to admit. Her body was solidly formed and supple—maybe about eighteen; her legs, well shaped below the midnight-blue skirt. Yes, there was no doubt about it, he told himself. Life could be tough at times.

CHAPTER SEVENTEEN

THEY got to meet with their assigned coach every other day on average, typically for fifteen to thirty minutes. Mr. Summer had dark hair and a sallow face with a mustache, and exuded an odor of tobacco although he didn't use it publicly. He cut less of an athletic image than Mr. Green at Coulie had, but that was maybe to be expected in view of the different nature of Seville Trace. His manner had a certain shortness and directness, but he seemed competent enough at what he did and was fair-minded in his treatment of those put in his charge, which was the main thing. However, when he and Linc next met in one of the offices for their scheduled review session, Linc sensed a reserve about him that hadn't been there previously.

"There was an accident in the tool store yesterday," Mr. Summer said.

"You mean Welsh?" Linc nodded. "Yes, I know about it." The handle had come off a case of heavy jig blocks when Welsh lifted it from a shelf. The case had dropped, scraping his shin and badly bruising a foot.

"Welsh thinks the screws holding the handle must have been loosened," Mr. Summer said.

Linc sighed. From the look in Mr. Summer's eye, it was clear who had been suggested as having perhaps done the loosening. It was clear enough to Linc what had happened: There had been an accident, and somebody had used it as an opportunity to spread rumors. He shook his head, showing his hands. "How could anyone tell? . . . Things like that happen."

But Mr. Summer was evidently not satisfied to just pass it off. "We all know that Welsh is a buddy of Arvin's," he said. "And you've been having this feud going with Arvin ever since you both got here. They've been giving you a hard time, haven't they, in one way and another? . . ." The implication was plain. Mr. Summer let it hang.

Simply denying it would have been pointless, since Linc would be expected to do so. And protesting would have sounded too much like whining. In the end Linc let it go with, "Look, if I was going to risk blowing things, I'd be sure to make it over something a little more worthwhile than that."

The answer seemed to allay Mr. Summer's suspicions somewhat. He nodded. "I'd like to think you're right, Linc. You're a lot more intelligent than you perhaps realize. But you do have this history of violence to live down. It would be a tragedy to see you spoil things now. Let's see how you do with the practical tests tomorrow."

After the previous incident, Mr. Throw seemed to have been arranging his timetable to keep Linc and Arvin apart. On the afternoon following the day of Linc's talk with Mr. Summer, however, Arvin was slotted into the same class as Linc when the evening session was canceled to free up the gym space for another event. Inevitably, when the time came for sparring and partners rotated, they ended up facing each other once again. Conceivably, Mr. Throw could have intervened and separated them, but it would have created an ungainly situation by focusing attention on something he was trying to play down—and no doubt would have preferred not to have to acknowledge existed at all. In any event, his response was to simply let things run.

The contest between Linc and Arvin degenerated into a tussle that got dirty and then went downhill from there. Arvin made a habit of dropping to the mat while hanging onto Linc's jacket, dragging Linc down to continue by means of ground fighting, where Arvin's weight gave him an edge. In this, he was particularly ferocious in trying to apply armlocks, which Linc became equally violent at avoiding—another "accident" like last time, he quickly perceived, would put him in a cast for a month. His anger rising, Linc retaliated with savagely effective choke holds, sustaining the pressure for several seconds after Arvin's submission signal, leaving him red-faced and gasping. The rancor between them could be felt by the rest of the class, who grew less vocal and were clearly uncomfortable. By the time the session ended, Mr. Throw was exasperated and ready to take both of them on personally.

"Not Linc and Arvin," he called, when he dismissed the others. "You two stay behind." They stood, eyeing each other coldly while Mr. Throw closed the door behind the last of the departing figures. He turned and came back across the mat to where they were standing. "All right," he told them in a tight voice. "I don't know what this is all about, but it's affecting my class, so let's have it out and get rid of it. This is *off* the record, understand? What happens here right now never happened. Your own rules apply unless I say different. Got it?"

Linc felt his instincts taking control. A hundred experiences had taught him the advantage of just letting his body react in situations like this, when his mind wanted to think for a split second longer. That split second could make the difference. Most men lost through giving in to that impulse to hold off for just a moment, to be sure—which allowed events to drive them, instead of the other way around.

Mr. Throw held up an arm like a starter at a race. "Now, back off three paces, each of you. . . ." Linc exhaled hard, and then opened his mouth wide, sucking in a last-moment lungful of oxygen. "Ready. . . . *Go!*"

Linc flew. There was no sizing up or holding back to get any measure. Arvin had barely moved or even registered that anything had started to happen when the first punch hit him full on the jaw. Linc followed it with a second, third, fourth . . . ten staccato blows into the face with the same fist, too fast even to allow pause for changing hands. Arvin was glazed and bewildered even before the last had shot home. Linc slammed a foot into his stomach as his guard flopped, doubling him over, and clubbed him to the floor with three hammer fists using the other hand, delivered to the back of his head and neck. For an instant he saw in the blond waves not Arvin but Kyle, and his impulse was to finish things with kicks to the side of the body; but there was no need, and he held off—turning away, instead, contemptuously.

Even Mr. Throw seemed taken aback by the speed and violence of the attack. He went down on one knee and turned Arvin's head up to check him. Although not KO'd, he was functionally out of things, his eyes rolled upward, face marked and bloody, nose streaming—Linc had made sure not to omit that.

"*Jeez!*" Mr. Throw muttered softly. "I guess we can take it that you've been around some?"

Breathing heavily, Linc picked up a towel. His first reaction was a surge of inner satisfaction. After days, weeks, of the tension that had been building up in side him, the release was worth whatever happened now. He didn't care what they did. A few moments later, after he had mopped his face and the adrenaline hit began to subside, he was less sure. He looked at Mr. Throw questioningly. "Is that it? You meant what you said? This doesn't make any difference to anything, right?"

Mr. Throw nodded slowly, not quite able to keep a hint of

awe out of his gaze. “We never go back on our word here,” he said.

Linc nodded, slung the towel over his shoulder, and turned for the door.

Linc found he had good feelings inside that persisted through to the next day. By the day’s end they were even better. Although some of the calculations had been a bit tricky, he felt he hadn’t done too badly at all on the tests.

CHAPTER EIGHTEEN

ONLY the coaches seemed blind to the signs of Arvin's apparent encounter with a threshing machine. It didn't pass without notice, either, that the harassment Linc had been subjected to miraculously ceased. But that had no sooner become a topic of conversation when, two weeks before the end of the stay at Seville Trace, it was eclipsed by the announcement of a general address to be given the next day in the dining area, which because of the seating also doubled as the main auditorium. All classes and other activities were suspended. Everyone was to attend. Rumors immediately began circulating that it had to be the long-awaited revelation of what the program had been preparing the inmates for. For the rest of the day there was little talk that didn't lead back to airing all the standard theories yet again, with occasional new variations. Johnny thought they were being graded for high-skills potential to be sold off to other governments—commanding much better prices than unassessed raw labor, which lesser developed countries had no shortage of anyway. One of Marlene's friends suggested it could be for breeding experiments, which raised a few intriguing and imaginative speculations among some.

The buzz was approaching fever intensity by the time the remains of the late breakfast shift were disposed of, and those who had been elsewhere began arriving to swell the numbers. The Director was there, as expected, along with most of the staff. A number of visitors also showed up for the occasion. Among them, Linc was intrigued to note, with his white hair, bushy eyebrows, and heavy spectacles, still sporting a jacket and bow tie, was Dr. Grober. A number of Linc's colleagues recognized him too. Dr. Grober was evidently a busy man.

It turned out that Linc and those who had been thinking along similar lines as he were close to the truth. The intention was to send them out into space. Or, it would have been more accurate to say, "bring" them out into space. For, as the Director informed the packed room, by then completely hushed:

"The operation that I represent—along with the others of us that you've met since joining this program—is not a creation of government or any corporation, as many of you have been speculating. In fact, we are not from any organization with Earth-based loyalties at all. What we are from is the future." He paused for a moment and nodded at the puzzled looks he knew that would bring. "We are from the only real future that anyone has—the only future that there is for every one of you, the only future that there is for humanity. Specifically, we are from those regions, mostly extending outward beyond the orbit of Mars, that are generally referred to as the Outzone."

There were whistles, murmurs, stares of surprise and wonder, even though going out to space had been one of the possibilities bandied around interminably. But everyone contemplating it had for some reason fixated on the Earth-based alternatives.

Some of those around Linc nudged him or sent nods regardless, as if endorsing him as one of the few who had gotten it right.

Like most of them, Linc was not unaware of the human presence in the Outzone, but he had no idea of the purpose, paying as little attention to the subject as he had to other activities in space and the rest of things that didn't impact his immediate life. The media coverage was usually scornful, treating it as an escape for dreamers and diversion of energies from more important issues closer to home, and people talked about it usually with amusement, as if it were a kind of joke. The Director seemed to have anticipated such reactions, for he continued:

"Let me put you straight about some of the things you've all doubtless heard. What's going on out there is new, something different from anything that's happened before in human history. We're seeing the beginnings of a society built around ideas of human relationships that are different from the ones you're used to—so different, in fact, that your first feelings might be that they don't make sense. Let me list a few. Command through loyalty, not authority. Respect in place of fear. Competence and knowledge, the only true wealth." The Director looked around at their expression as they puzzled over the words. He gave them several seconds and then explained, "Because out where we are, you can't afford to waste human talent. You have to harness the potential that exists in *everyone* for doing something worthwhile and being needed. There isn't any room for passengers. And in particular, there is no room for a mass of unthinking, obedient sheep, whose only function is to be exploited and controlled by a privileged few. Everyone must be free to become the most they are capable of."

Such a line was totally new to those listening. An unusual stillness had taken over the room. The Director made a brief, dismissive motion with a hand.

"Forget all the ideas about government and about corporations that you've been carrying around in your heads. Forget what you've been told by the people who create and control such organizations, and by those who serve them, about how life is and how it just has to be. *Nothing* 'just has' to be. *You* . . ." the Director pointed, singling out one of the listeners near the front, then moved his arm and his eyes in a slow circle to bring in all of them—"are the most creative and productive creature ever to appear on the surface of this planet. You built cities, wrote symphonies, turned deserts into gardens, and invented machines that fly. You have the ability inside—all of you, every one—to make life any way you want."

Still extending his finger, the Director raised his arm until it pointed upward.

"Out there a new culture is coming into existence, based on values that are different from the ones you've spent your lives having drummed into you. Oh, they've been talked about for centuries, sure enough, but more lately they seem to have been forgotten. In forgetting them, Earth created conditions that allowed no place for people like you, sitting here—and then it told you it has no use for you, that you're no good. We from the Outzone don't agree. To us, every kind of skill and ability is priceless. We can use every one of you in this room, and as many more as they care to send, for as long as Earth is happy to have its 'misfits' and 'undesirables' taken off its hands. . . ." A crooked smile lightened the Director's expression for just a second. "And if they want to laugh and think we're a little crazy, well, that's just fine by us too." The moment was well timed and produced smiles. Linc found an excitement rising inside as he heard thoughts and feelings at last being voiced that expressed what he had been waiting for without knowing it. The Director had them all coming around to him now. He moved out to them a few paces, as if drawing them nearer. His voice fell to a more personal, conversational note.

"Let me tell you a little about the way I see things today. Earth is suffering from stagnation of the spirit. The whole focus of its energies, indeed its entire awareness, is on the immediate, the material—to the point that nothing else has come to have any meaning or even to exist. Mankind has lost the ability to dream—to dream the kind of dreams that built nations and civilizations. People no longer know what it means to work together toward a shared vision of something larger than any of them, that will last longer than all of them, and make every individual life that contributed to it that much more worthwhile." The Director's mouth curled distastefully for a moment. "Instead . . . what do we have? A war of all preying upon all. Everyone hostile and alienated, each using everyone else for whatever's up for grabs. You've all heard it every day: 'What do *I* get out of it, *now?*'"

He made an empty-handed gesture.

"The problems that have paralyzed the world are diseases of the mind—products of deluded imaginations that see only too many people running out of room and resources, and not enough for them to do. That's what they're telling you. The future that *we* are building, by contrast, promises infinite room with unlimited resources. And there could *never* be enough people for all the things out there that will need to be done."

He paused at that point and looked around, as if to give them a few moments to absorb what he had said. But there was little movement or sound. They were hungry for more. He resumed:

"I suppose you're all waiting for the catch. There has to be one, of course. . . . Except that, after you've had some more practice at thinking and seeing things in the way I'm talking about, maybe you will come to view it as not so much of a catch after all. But what might seem like one for the moment is that we Outzoners entangle ourselves as little as possible in the political and economic affairs of Earth. Therefore, we can't offer much in the way of what you are accustomed to think of as payment. But then, the concept of individual wealth doesn't mean very much out there, in any case. The only 'wealth' that has any significance is what I alluded to a few minutes ago: the skills and knowledge you contribute to help create the technologies and other assets that secure the enterprise as a whole. *That* is how people are rated and what they're rewarded for. The reward is freedom to become whatever you choose and are capable of—the only true freedom that matters—and to be valued for that, and that alone.

"And now I'm going to use language you don't hear every

day. What we offer is opportunity: the opportunity to *serve*, not a chance of obtaining privileges; the opportunity to honor *obligation*, not demand rights. What obligation? The obligation to return the best you are capable of to others, whose doing likewise makes the existence of all of us possible. Cooperation to the utmost degree is what matters out there. Survival itself depends on it. Anything less would equate to mutual destruction—which is what Earth has chosen." The Director turned to take in the whole room with an appealing gesture. "And for the past three months every one of you present in this room has, in a limited way, been practicing just these things I've described. And it appears that, as seems to be true more often than not of younger people, such a philosophy and worldview suits your nature. . . . Which, of course, is why you are here."

This was so unlike everything Linc was used to hearing repeated all around him every day and had never questioned that it was almost like listening to a strange language. Yet at the same time the words had a deeply stirring effect, articulating so closely things he realized he had *wanted* to believe but had never seen in the reality he'd always lived in, and which he had therefore concluded couldn't exist. Now he was hearing not only that they could, but they *did*, exist; this time he would be there. And all of a sudden he was impatient. He wanted to be out there now, to become a part of it. And more than that, he realized. It wasn't enough just to *be* a part of it. He wanted to *give* something to it, to put a part of himself into making it happen. For the first time in his life, he saw a way of doing and being something worthwhile.

The hall had become very still and quiet. Looking around, he saw that others seemed to be affected in the same kind of way. Not all of them—in some places there were frowns, shakings of heads, exchanges of looks that said *not me*. But the majority, *yes!* Rocky's lanky frame was leaned back, tilting his chair, his face a picture of distant wonder. Johnny and Patch gave each other thumbs-ups beside him. A couple of tables away, a girl sitting behind Mace leaned forward to punch him on the shoulder, as if to say *Hear that!* Mace turned his head, nodded, and grinned. Flash was jerking his head to look from one to another of the coaches, as if seeing them in a new light suddenly. Then Arvin, his face still showing bruises, caught Linc's eye from across the room; and just for an instant something communicated itself between them that was devoid of malice. . . . And then Arvin's expression darkened, and he looked away again quickly.

But that was fine by Linc. Arvin no longer troubled him. Now, suddenly, there was a whole new future to think about.

CHAPTER NINETEEN

THE Director had given the general picture. It was expected that most of those listening would want to talk more with their coaches before reaching a decision. That was why the announcement had been made a week before the time at Seville Trace was up. To Linc, the appeal of what had been described was such that he had difficulty visualizing how anyone could turn it down. But once again, the end of the phase marked a moment of high attrition. Some, it appeared, weren't swayed by the same kinds of images as he, and preferred to take the chances that came with the familiar patterns of life. Others just had an unallayable suspicion that they hadn't been told everything and there had to be a downside. And there were those who shrunk from the thought of being immersed in newness, farther away than they were capable of comprehending from everything they knew. They would stay with the known, even if not entirely trusted, whatever the consequences. But all who chose to go at this stage were accepted. Nobody was dropped by a decision of the authorities. As Mr. Summer explained when Linc finally got to see him late in the afternoon of the day following the Director's announcement:

"We're not recruiting for some elite unit of the army or anything like that. We have the beginnings of a whole society taking shape. New people are going to be born there—in fact, they are being born already—and that means as varied as people come. A society that couldn't absorb all kinds wouldn't be much use. Is it supposed to eliminate the ones who don't fit? Society should be shaped to fit people the way they are. It's trying to do it the other way that causes the problems."

"What about the ones who were RPO'd?" Linc asked. "How come you couldn't absorb them? Or don't they count for some reason?"

They were using one of the admin offices, Mr. Summer at the desk, Linc in a chair pulled up opposite. The next two of Mr. Summer's charges scheduled for sessions that afternoon were waiting outside. With six rooms to take care of, and four occupants to a room—less the dropouts—he had been busy like this all day.

"That wasn't the same thing," Mr. Summer replied. "They were elements that would have disrupted the course. It wasn't a reflection of whether or not we could have accommodated them eventually. Even a tree sometimes needs help getting started. We don't have unlimited time—as I'm sure you're only too aware by now."

Linc stared at the desktop. It was almost bare, with just a thickish file folder that Linc assumed pertained to him but which hadn't been referred to, and a notepad on which Mr. Summer had jotted a few lines. There was only one other thing Linc could think of. "Who pays?" he asked, looking up. "I men, all this here. . . ." He swept a hand, indicating the surroundings. "The other place I was at. The Director said you don't have much to do with Earth economically. So who owns it all?"

"You care?" Mr. Summer sounded surprised.

Linc shrugged. "Just kinda curious, I guess."

"You could think of it as a leasing of a kind. We have certain arrangements with state and federal authorities. As the Director indicated yesterday, they view it as unloading unwanted merchandise." Mr. Summer's face twitched in a quick, humorless smile. "You're probably aware that most of the world thinks of us as wildly unrealistic—simpleminded even. If that's the image they choose to create—because it lets them off the hook of having to think too hard about the way they're heading, maybe—that's okay by us. As the Director also said, we'll continue to take whatever they send, for as long as they want to carry on believing they're pulling one over on us."

The logic appealed to Linc, and he smiled faintly. That in itself was an indicator of the effects of the past three months; that time ago he had never smiled at anything. Mr. Summer took it as a good moment to wrap up the interview. "So," he said, resting his chin on his interlaced fingers and staring over them, "do I take it that you're in? You're signing up for the ride?"

Linc nodded. "Oh, sure. I thought that was already understood." He expected his tone of finality would be the end of it. But the way Mr. Summer continued staring at him told him there was more. "What? . . ." he asked.

Mr. Summer opened the file finally, and then sat looking at it for a few seconds, as if composing something in his mind that was not easy to say. Linc waited. "Of course there's no question that you'll go . . ." Mr. Summer began. "But I'm afraid the news I have isn't all good."

The utterance caught Linc unprepared. The past three months had, to a degree, mellowed his former cynicism. Things seemed to have gone well, and inwardly he had felt pride in the unsuspected parts of his personality he was beginning to uncover. He had hoped to hear positive things—encouragement, maybe a little praise even. . . .

"The results of your machining tests weren't great," Mr.

Summer continued. "They're not up to the proficiency level that the engineering people need to see. I know that the subject has an appeal for you, Linc. But . . ." Mr. Summer made a resigned gesture, "wanting something isn't always enough. What we have here doesn't point to a future in that particular direction. I'm sorry."

Linc was too dazed to think coherently. That was the last area in which he had expected to hear criticism. "I thought I did okay," was all he could manage. His voice came out flat and feeble. It sounded lame.

"The dimensional calculations were all off. . . ." Mr. Summer searched for a way to soften the blow. "Look, it doesn't necessarily mean the end of the line. You won't be denied access to further opportunity to develop that kind of talent—if it's what you really want to do. But for now . . ." Mr. Summer waved a hand and left the rest unsaid.

Linc's first impulse as the initial numbness passed was anger—the conditioning of a life that had conspired to thwart him at the last moment whenever anything started looking as if it were going well. He had tried as hard as anyone could in an environment that was new and strange to him. What more did they want? The injustice made him want to smash something, throw something, upend the desk into Mr. Summer's sick-making, pretending-that-he-gave-a-damn face. . . . But something else had happened, also, in those three months that let him see the futility of giving way to such feelings, and he fought them down with a power of restraint he hadn't possessed previously. There was no way now that he could go back to where he had come from. He couldn't afford to leave himself with nowhere to go forward to either.

"What, then?" he asked woodenly.

Mr. Summer sat forward, mustering an expression intended to be optimistic. "Let's look at the strengths you do have," he suggested. "You're physically tough and superbly coordinated. You think fast, and you're hardly a wimp, as our friend Arvin will testify. And experience here and at Coulie shows you have a natural leadership quality that others will respond to and follow. I'd like you to consider, instead, the thought of becoming a professional in the military or security services. We think you're cut out for it. Your earlier background might even constitute something of an asset that you could put to use. It gives you a good slant on assessing certain personalities and situations."

Linc's first reaction was to scoff. "Military? Out past Mars? Who are you thinking of taking on out there? Have people been seeing little green guys or something?"

Mr. Summer remained serious. "Don't go running away with any wrong ideas, Linc. As the Director said yesterday, if Earth wants to treat the Outzone culture as some kind of joke, that's fine by us for as long as it lasts, because it gives us more time. But we are bringing together some exceptionally capable people out there—scientists, engineers, builders, and creators of all kinds, who have been quietly disappearing. People who are sick of the greed and the exploitation, and a society that pays lip service to truth and honesty while heaping its rewards on the most accomplished forms of lying and robbery. When people like that are free, they can achieve astounding results. Whole new areas of science are being opened up out there—discoveries that Earth has lost the will and the ability to make anymore. When Earth wakes up to what's going on, there's a good chance it will try to get a share in the only way it knows how: by claims of 'rights' and enforcing them through violence. The Outzone may have to defend itself. If it does, it will need people like you. And that's why we're happy to take all the time we can get."

Suddenly, Linc felt very weary—the debilitating, exhausting weariness that comes with the realization that one's best isn't enough. His weight seemed to compress him down into the chair. "So what was all that stuff Grober told me up front?" he said, unable to keep the bitterness out of his voice. "He said we were supposed to have a choice in all this. What happened to that?"

"The choice was to come with us or go back," Mr. Summer replied. "And it still stands. But one of the things implied in choosing us is agreeing to accept orders from those judged qualified to give them. As you'll find out for yourself—I hope you'll stick around to find out—it's the only way things can function out there. For a long time yet, at least."

This time there was a celebration to mark the completion of the phase: A party and a dance were announced for the second-to-last night. The main hall was spruced up and decorated for the occasion. The best caterers that the course had produced excelled themselves in finding appropriate dishes and delicacies. A brown-skinned kid called Muddy (he was presumably from Mississippi) did a creditable job as deejay, and others who fancied their talents took turns at rendering live vocals. All in all, things moved and swung pretty well. In one of those unspoken understandings that can telegraph itself through groups without pinpointable origins, the fraternization ban was sensed as effectively inoperative. A major part of the hard work was finally complete, and easing up was in order. The coaches were looking the other way.

Linc's feelings toward the affair were mixed. He was glad for these past three months, yet disappointed; excited and at the same time mildly apprehensive about the future. Although the center of the group that usually clustered around him, he was unable to lose himself to the spirit of things. He grinned approvingly at Patch's and Johnny's antics on the dance floor with their partners, but didn't join in. He winked as Rocky was about to slip away hand in hand with Liz but declined to respond to the hints being sent, sometimes none too subtly, in his direction by some of the other girls. Finally, holding a can of the "frail-ale" nonalcoholic brew that had been brought in to impart atmosphere, he sauntered outside on his own to the pool area to get some relief from the noise. There were others scattered around who seemed to have had the same idea, he saw as he came out into the cool of the night. Okay than, not quite on his own; but at least he would have a few minutes of uncrowded space.

Marlene appeared beside him before he had savored a first lungful of the air. Linc wasn't sure if she had followed him or been out there already. She looked fresh and feminine out of uniform, in one of the dresses that had appeared from somewhere—a yellow one. Linc eyed her mutely, not volunteering conversation. She had sought him out; let her start it.

"Not partying then, Linc?" she said.

"Oh . . . just taking a break from it, I guess."

"It gets kind of close in there, doesn't it?"

"That's what I figured."

"Yeah. Me too." Marlene gave that funny kind of laugh that said isn't it strange: We both thought the same thing. "So did you come out looking for some company?" Linc sighed inwardly, anticipating a proposition again and already searching in his mind for the right way to steer her off. He really wasn't in the mood. But then he saw that she was looking around and not especially listening for his reply. Even before he could frame one, she went on, "I'd like to oblige, but I'm already . . . You know how it is."

So that was it. She just *had* to let him know.

As if on cue, Arvin appeared through the same door that Linc had come out of. Arvin stiffened for a moment when he saw them, then came over and took Marlene's arm firmly, with a defiant look, as if claiming a possession. Linc looked back neutrally, asserting or conceding nothing, not involved and not wanting to be. Marlene shot a haughty look back at him as they walked away in the shadows by the building, turning away as Arvin pulled her after him. "What the hell are you doing around him?" Linc heard Arvin mutter. It would end in a fight, he could sense. He turned his back on them and moved toward the pool.

The water was calm, reflecting the Moon and stars in a cloudless sky. Linc raised his head to stare up at them. Restlessness came over him again. Always, it seemed, he was turning his back on one phase of life, waiting impatiently to move on to another. He wondered if he would ever belong in any of them.

CHAPTER TWENTY

IT seemed that the Outzoners made a business out of taking over assets that Earth-based interests had judged unprofitable by their own measures of worth, and abandoned. Camp Coulie had once trained units of the military—now being scaled down and reformed to merge into a global police force with the move toward an eventual world government. Seville Trace, intended as a hotel, had been obsoleted by other technologies in the ceaseless pursuit of trying to get more for less. Meyer Flat, in Colorado, it turned out, had previously been a small community college, since closed down because of funding cutbacks.

Grayling Station, named after somebody otherwise forgotten to most, who had been involved with its conception, had been built as a collection port for payloads of moon rock catapulted electromagnetically into orbit from mining operations on the lunar surface. From there, according to the original plan, the ores and other materials would be distributed by transporter vessels to various construction enterprises planned to take shape across the nearby regions of space. When the ventures ran into unanticipated obstacles and complications, however, the major investors had pulled out, redirecting their funds into areas of proven safer returns, presumably more highly valued by Earth society, such as cosmetic gene therapy and mood-sensitive entertainments. These days the Outzoners used Grayling Station as a first-step training base for their recruits before sending them on to the reaches of deeper space. The governments who supplied many of the recruits showed the calculated savings as income on their balance sheets, paid a portion of it as risk-free return to the original investors, and that way everyone was happy.

The station hung in the L_2 libration point, three hundred thousand miles away from Earth, directly in line on the far side of the Moon—a choice reflecting its originally intended function. This, Linc had learned during a five-day familiarization course at a technical center near the launch facility on Yucatán, was one of five points in the Earth-Moon vicinity where the effects of both gravities and the centrifugal orbiting force cancel out, enabling a body to remain in the same relative position. (It was one of three unstable points of the five, meaning that an object placed there would tend to drift. Jets were therefore fired periodically to nudge the station back into position.)

His first view of the structure, not counting the models and diagrams he had studied as part of the preparation, was on the cabin wall-screen in a transfer shuttle closing in on the station two days after liftoff and separation from the booster that had carried it to Low Earth Orbit. Its general form was that of a pair of crossed barbells. The "bars" consisted of tube-and-latticework booms several hundred feet long projecting from a roughly cylindrical central assembly that included docking facilities at one end and a nuclear generating plant at the other, forming an oversize "axle." Cylinders at the ends of the bars, made up of various living, working, and functional areas stacked like disks, formed the "weights" at the ends of the bars. Slow rotation of the whole produced a simulated gravity effect perpendicular to the floors inside the peripheral cylinders. A web of ties, lines, and assorted structural additions had grown between the booms, and a gaggle of outstations serving various purposes moved with the main structure in a loose formation spread through a volume of space fifty or more miles across. One of the larger of these, called Jade, had a transparent outer skin filled with water as its radiation and thermal shield, and making it also the emergency water reserve for the whole complex of stations. Algae cultured in the shield for hydroponics processing and biological experiments gave a green tint through which starlight diffused, causing it to shine eerily like a gemstone in the heavens. One of the speakers who came to address Linc's group at Yucatán—they were officially *recruits* now, not *inmates* or *guests*—offered the thought that one indication of intelligent life spreading across distant galaxies might be the greening of light from their constituent stars.

Life had become less programmed and structured. There was no formally defined Phase Three for everyone to move on to as had been the case with the transition from Phase One. Different groups and individuals went different ways to prepare for the different futures that ability, preference, need, and an inevitable element of chance had concocted for them.

Probably because overt military training was not considered a wise thing to flaunt on Earth, Linc had been part of an advance group sent to Yucatán for immediate transfer up to Grayling. Included as well in the same group of early birds were Arvin, also earmarked as natural for the military; Flash, now Linc's solid ally and buddy, with ambitions to develop his technical abilities in a military direction; and Rocky, who had volunteered because of lack of inspiration for anything else. Mace was one of those selected for training as space-construction riggers, who were going up early to get preliminary experience at Grayling. Also included was Liz, who had shown little inclination toward anything beyond routine office chores but somehow wangled things to be near Rocky.

Linc had come to accept Patch as the strongest friend he had known since Angelo, and in their conversations had opened up to him in a way that was rare. He had hoped that Patch would be singled out for something that would involve early shipment too and keep them together, but circumstances didn't work out that way. A couple of the Seville Trace coaches talked to Patch at length about his mountaineering experiences and general interest in remote regions, and he was spirited away a day or two later. He and Linc reaffirmed their promise that they would go climbing together again on Earth one day.

Another face that Linc had gotten used to but which went a separate way, was "Piano Man" Johnny. His outspoken politics, which would have branded him as a subversive and gotten him locked up in most other places, were evidently viewed differently here. He'd been told he was being sent on a crash college course somewhere. One person Linc didn't miss was Welsh, his antagonist from the machining tool store, who exercised his right to opt out and left the scene permanently. So once again, Arvin was left without a willing sidekick to report happenings and run errands.

Unlike previously, the people that Linc and the others found themselves among at Yucatán were not all of younger age groups, and from their talk and manner it quickly became apparent that they came from all kinds of backgrounds. There were loners looking for a new start; family groups ready to leave all in search of what they saw as freedom; professionals seeking recognition that eluded them in the exploitive jungles that Earth had become. Linc met two engineers from places in Siberia that he'd never heard of, going out to work in the plants that processed materials out of asteroids. There was a Chinese kid his own age whose whole family had been lost in the civil war going on there. A schoolteacher and her husband from Iraq—wherever that was—who were getting away to start a family. Although there was no particular reason why not, it had never before crossed Linc's mind that the operation might extend beyond the U.S. borders. The Outzone was obviously eager for all that Earth had to offer.

This was no longer a reorientation and redirection program for salvaged delinquents. For those who had come via the same route as Linc, the ban on talking about past lives was lifted. The past was of little significance now. Also, they were free at last to use their full names. The common visions all of them would be sharing from here onward were to the future.

CHAPTER TWENTY-ONE

THE main function of Grayling Station was to provide a first taste of living and working in space. Nobody wanted to be whisked out to somewhere like the moons of Jupiter before realizing they weren't suited to it (or responsible for getting them back again!). Apart from the instructors and regular crew who ran the place, its population consisted of a temporary association of transients who would be going on to other things.

The central axlelike structure was known, understandably, as the Axle. The cylinders at the ends of the booms were called towers and designated North, East, South, and West, the normal convention applying to the structure when viewed such that it rotated clockwise. South Tower contained the command and communications center, or Bridge, along with the armory and garrison space for the military contingent. The military presence comprised both the station's permanent force and new recruits undergoing familiarization training, and occupied a set of decks and compartments located "below" (i.e., outward from) the Bridge, known collectively as the Turret.

Here was where Linc and his companions found themselves, once again picking bunks and unpacking belongings, in the quarters set aside for cadet troops. Their uniforms now were pale gray—military-style, like those of the former instructors. It was a very different environment from the previous ones, however—of cramped space and metal walls, where the floor throbbed to the hum of invisible machinery and the air smelled of hot oil. The company they found themselves among was different too from what they had become used to. Besides the wider range of ages, there was a watchfulness about the new faces around them that reminded Linc of the first days at Coulie—the silent assessment by people accustomed to possibly threatening situations, not yet sure of what to expect. Many of them had prior military backgrounds, he sensed—possibly from anywhere the world over. This could be a whole new chapter of learning experience.

And there was one face—one for the time being at least—that was familiar. When Linc, after stowing his kit in his new quarters, went to check out the general messroom in the hour of free time they had been given to get their bearings, a voice called out at him when he had barely entered the room. "Hey, don't tell me. . . . Yes, it is! Linc! Why am I not totally surprised to see you here?"

It was Little Mac from Coulie, turning away from a serving hatch in one wall. He was holding a plate of sausage, fries, and beans, and a mug of something hot, and looked as if he was about to join three other cadets at the end of one of the room's two long tables.

"Mackerel!" Linc shook his head. "I don't believe this! How long have you been here? . . . Where'd you come here from?"

"Since two days ago. Grab yourself some tea or something and sit down. . . . Guys, this is Linc, a buddy who was on the prep course I went through. Linc, these are Arch, Gus, and Willie. Hey, why not move along there and make a little room? . . ."

Linc took a tea and joined them at the end of the bench seat running along the wall. Arch and Gus had arrived with Mackerel from what sounded like another Phase Two that the other half from Coulie had been routed to—held somewhere near Boston. They both wore the blue mountain-peak shoulder patch that signified having gone through Phase One at Meyer Flat in Colorado, and they knew Rocky and the others when Linc mentioned them. Willie had come via an independent route not connected with the program. He said he'd joined the military-training scheme because it offered space-pilot training, and he was going to join an uncle who was in the Outzone already. The news on others Linc had known was that Big Mac had an academic flair that surprised everyone, and was hoping to go into engineering; someone in the Boston course had pulled a knife on Vic, but come out the worse for it and been RPO'd—Vic was okay; Kew had dropped out, apparently preferring an option that had to do with family connections. And, yes, in answer to Linc's question, Rick, who had bunked next to him at Coulie, had been at Boston too. . . . Mackerel wasn't sure what was happening with him.

Linc responded with high points of the news from Texas. Flash from Coulie had also opted for a technical line in the military and had come up with Linc. Mace was here too, or very soon would be, fixing to become a rigger. The big item that Mackerel might be interested in was that Arvin was not only in the cadet school as well, but had also been on the same shuttle. "In fact, he was sorting out his stuff on the billet deck downstairs when I left," Linc concluded. "He'll probably show up here in a few minutes."

"Jeez. . . . That's all we need," Mackerel said. He looked stunned.

"Who's Arvin?" Willie asked. He was mild mannered, with dark hair and a nervous smile. The obvious familiarity between the others was probably a little intimidating for him.

Mackerel waved a hand in the air. "Oh, big guy with a pretty blond wavy head, built like a truck. You'll know him when you see him."

"Is he the one on the climbing trip you were telling us about, Mac?" Gus asked. The one who . . ." He broke off and looked at Linc with sudden realization on his face. "*Linc!* You're the guy who had the standoff with the hard case and his two buddies. . . ."

"That's right. Vic was one of them," Arch interrupted.

Gus had dark coloring, a snub nose and wrinkly features permanently set in a thick-lipped frown as if experiencing a bad odor. "That Vic can be real mean when he wants." He nodded. "Yep. You've gotta be a natural for the army, Linc. Welcome aboard, man."

"Right. It's good to meet you." Arch thrust out an eager hand and smiled broadly, evidently impressed. He was lean with pinky eyes, like a rabbit's, and was sporting a wisp of a beard.

"So who's this Arvin?" Willie asked again.

"One of that kind who'll push you around if you let him," Mackerel said. "Just don't let him get away with it if he tries." Willie didn't look very happy.

"Don't look so worried. You'll be okay," Gus told him. "We'll look out for you. Right, guys?"

"As a matter of fact, I think you'll find he's mellowed out some since you last saw him," Linc confided, looking at Mackerel. A hint of mischief flickered in his eye, which he didn't try to hide.

"What happened?" Mackerel asked.

"Oh . . . you'll probably hear soon enough."

"Come on, Linc. What's wrong with now?"

At that moment another cadet uniform appeared in the doorway, and Rocky entered. This time it was Arch and Gus's turn to yell out in delight. "Forget about Arvin for now," Linc said to Mackerel. He motioned with his eyes and inclined his head. "Here's another guy that you have to meet. . . ."

• • •

The rest of the "day"—the regular twenty-four-hour period was observed, although it corresponded to no natural or other kind of cycle on Grayling—was taken up with introductory formalities and instruction on the command system and function of Grayling's military presence. Unlike the brief spell in Yucatán, where life had anticipated the freer pattern of the rest of the station, the routine in the Turret was styled upon military discipline and fastidiousness of detail. In some ways Linc's first impressions were that his existence had regressed from the quality it had attained at Coulie and Seville Trace to something more like the detention conditions he had known previously. A crop-headed sergeant called Schultz, who was in charge of cadet basic training, shouted incessantly and was satisfied by nothing. Every minor infraction became a reason for personal degradation and abuse. Linc gritted his teeth and reminded himself that he had chosen to accept it.

Late that night, in a brief relaxation period before lights-out, he made his way to one of the outer compartments with an observation window and stared silently at the panorama of space surrounding them. The day had been so busy that this was really the first chance he'd had to reflect on where he was, and actually to *feel* within himself something of what it meant. It was one of the few times in his life—maybe the first, truly—in which he had been conscious of a feeling of genuine awe.

He remembered how, up among the Sierra peaks, he had sat in the night with Patch, marveling that there could be so many stars, and so bright. But that had been nothing compared with this. Here, the night had a quality of infinite depth that no experience on Earth could ever capture, the stars and the voids between them brilliant with hues he had never dreamed existed. The whole, enormous constellation, a huge, half-lit Moon of unfamiliar surface markings in the foreground, wheeled before him on the far side of the rounded bulk of the Axle and the distant, foreshortened lines of the North Tower continuing beyond that. And Earth itself? Not a trace. Everything he had ever known, all the places he had been, as well as the thousands more never glimpsed and as many again never heard of—were eclipsed permanently on the far side of the Moon. All of it could have been swallowed in an instant by a universe that would never even notice.

Yet along with the wonder, there was a sense of loss—all the greater for having been so briefly glimpsed.

All around him were miracles worked in precise shapes of metal. Suddenly the shell enclosing him seemed very thin and fragile. His very life depended on the knowledge and skills of those who had designed and built it. People had once called him a brute, and he had believed them because that was all he had known. It had become his source of pride. Then others who knew powers of creating instead of destroying had shown him a part of himself that was better. That was what he had thought would grow and become a new person in a new life among the stars. Now, it seemed, he was to remain forever a destroyer. He wanted to believe that the callous verdict was wrong. But who was he to be so sure? And even if he convinced himself, why should he expect that it would change the minds of those who understood so much more?

Beyond the gleaming metallic lines of the North Tower, the Moon slid slowly upward, out of sight. Linc turned away and headed back to the billeting deck to bed down for his first night in space.

CHAPTER TWENTY-TWO

FOR the next four weeks the cadets underwent what was described as Accelerated Basic Training, during which time they were restricted to the Turret. Those like Willie, who were from regular backgrounds and had known the destination to which they were bound, had been through a preparatory course that sounded like a cut-down version of Coulie, so none of them were in what could be called poor condition; nevertheless, the routine involved a lot of weight pushing, and sweating on exercise machines to get in shape. There was no arguing with regulations. They learned about orders of rank and insignia, the functions of all standard items of kit and how to take care of them. They were introduced to hand-to-hand combat—dirtier than had been shown at Seville

Trace. There was interminable parade and small-arms drill of the traditional kind, conducted with small squads in conditions that bordered on comical in the limited space the military gym permitted. The only purpose in confining them to the Turret, since there really weren't that many places to go, seemed to be to impart an awareness that they were now under military orders. As more than one of the veterans they found themselves among told them, they would quickly discover that making sense was one of the last things that mattered.

"You come in here a rabble! By der time you leave Graylink Station, you vill be material that soldiers can be made from!" Schultz screamed at them in his European accent. He was somehow apelike, of indeterminate age, with a head that was bald except for a fringe of reddish curls at the sides and back, and a mustache that curled up at the ends. Linc went through the required motions unprotesting, yet inwardly he found the machinations to instill discipline through intimidation pretty transparent and not very compelling as far as inspiring fear and terror went. Obviously, there were built-in limits that made the system a charade. It seemed to have its desired effect on the kids from more normal backgrounds, nevertheless. But they had probably never been screamed at in earnest by anyone in their lives before; and certainly they had never been visited by an arm man delivering a reminder, or had to deal with a blade waver who had boiled over on dope.

There were more classes in basic math and physics—pitched below the abilities of the majority of the cadets, but again regulations allowed no exemptions. A minimum level of knowledge was required that it was essential everyone be brought up to. It formed the prerequisite for understanding at least the basics of such things as static mechanics, kinetics and orbital dynamics, heat, and the behavior of fluids, without which meaningful adaptation to the space environment would be impossible. There was an introduction to computers and communications, because the effectiveness of every modern fighting force from five-man fire team to army division depended on the availability and quality of information. And there was instruction in weapons, ammunition, and explosives, because those were the basic tools of the trade that everyone was now in.

Linc had never dreamed that human ingenuity could conceive and perfect so many ways of killing people. Available to the individual combat soldier was a range of categories and calibers of guns able to inflict every form of abuse imaginable on the human body via projectiles that ranged from "clean" hole drillers and shot, to bullets that spread or shattered, excavating bone and tissue by the shovelful, bullets that exploded, and flying blenders capable of taking off an arm. In addition, there were grenades that splintered or ignited; mines that disabled, disemboweled, or dismembered; antitank, antiair munitions and rockets; flamethrowers, trench cudgels, bayonets, and knives. Places and people, he discovered, were not bombed but instead "took ordnance." *Ordnance*—explosive, incendiary, fragmentation, chemical, biological, nuclear; delivered by artillery, missile, air, orbiting platform—could single out a vehicle in a column, obliterate an area, incinerate a town. Laser cannons on the Moon tracked Earth-circling satellites. Beams of atomic particles could melt ships out in space.

The other cadets seemed intrigued and excited by it all, airing their new jargon over meals and enthusiastically debating infantry techniques and weapon specifications in their billet at the day's end. Linc found it disillusioning and depressing. For the most part the cadets were products of affluence and security trying to prove themselves—children raised on delusions of manly virtues and movie heroics. Linc had seen the effects of a broken bottle twisted into a human face, and a hand being pulped by a solid-iron bar. He had thought he was getting away from such things; that he had found a breed of people who were smarter and knew enough to be beyond living that way, and who would show him how to become one of them. But if they were that smart, why were they incapable, and on such a total and massive scale, of solving their problems and getting along with one another?

In his few years he hadn't found out too much about the world. He had always figured that people like himself lived violently and ruthlessly because it was the only way they had of getting a chance to carve themselves a share of anything—which was how he'd been conned into working for Kyle. Or, like Clay and Slam, the two punks he had hired, they didn't and never would know any different. Now he was coming to the conclusion that this wasn't the way it was after all, that there was a lot more to it. The smart ones were the worst: throwing kids in the slammer for leaning on a few jerks in order to get a decent car and a suit, while themselves looting nations wholesale and counting the corpses in millions. For the first time a lot of the things he remembered Johnny saying back at Seville Trace started to make sense. Linc wondered if this whole business was just another con, and at the end of it nothing was going to turn out any different from the way things always did. If so, he found himself thinking, he was never going to fit in anywhere.

CHAPTER TWENTY-THREE

LINC adjusted the shower to a cooler setting and let the water flow over his face and chest, carrying away the last of an hour's worth of pressing, pulling, and stretching, followed by three simulated miles on the running mill. The time when he'd felt stiff and achy was long past now. His body had the satisfying feel of well-toned muscles exercised thoroughly but easily within their limits. He pushed his hair back to clear his eyes and stared for a moment at the jets streaming out from the nozzle, trying to convince himself that the water wasn't really falling but moving in a straight line while the floor's rotation carried him in a curve to intercept it. It was no good. He couldn't visualize it that way. He had lived all his life and formed his conceptions in real gravity, and that was the end of it. He thought instead about the prospect of leave finally, after four weeks of continuous grind in the Turret. Only two more days to go. Then, an escape, finally, to whatever the rest of the station had to offer. And after that, life should get more interesting. When they returned to duty, they'd be going on to suits and the actual space environment—getting their first taste of spacewalking and activity outside, learning something of what was involved in building and repairing structures.

Knowing about structures was important in space. Everything that Earth had once been naturally was now replaced by artificial structures that weren't indestructible, didn't self-renew, and into which everything needed had to be deliberately designed. Structures kept you close to the things you needed to stay alive, and separated you from everything else in the universe that was trying to see you dead. And in space there was nowhere for soldiers to dig foxholes and trenches to feel safer in. They built structures.

"Feels good, eh, Linc?" Mackerel's voice came from the next stall.

"You said it."

"How much did you clock on the mill just before we quit?" one of the others who were toweling off outside called.

"Just over three," Linc threw back.

"Pretty good time then," Mackerel said.

"Not bad." Linc cut off the water and ran a hand over his head to squeeze out the excess.

"You know what occurred to me," Gus said as Linc stepped out. "They recycle everything up here. . . . Where do you suppose this water might have been yesterday?"

"Take a break, Gus. I don't want to think about it."

Arch switched at Gus with his towel. "You've got leave coming up in two days, man. Think positive things."

"All the big-city lights of the Axle," someone at the other end said.

"Center of the inhabited regions of the galaxy."

"Big deal."

"Which part of town are you planning on hitting first, Linc?" Arch asked.

"That's a tough one. I'll have to think about it."

"Where do they keep all the girls? It has to be the rec deck. That's where I'll be heading." Arch meant the Recreation Deck, located in the West Tower.

"Girls? . . . What are they?"

"You know—curvy things that look like centerfolds."

"Oh, those. Yeah, I think I remember."

"You vill conduct yourselves as soldiers," somebody threw in, imitating Schultz.

"Damn right!"

Linc put on a pair of long fatigue pants and a T-shirt, then collected his gear and left to return to the billet. Willie joined him as he began heading along the corridor outside. Although those like Linc—the ex-delinquents—were no longer required to conceal their backgrounds, the habit had become automatic. As a result, they inclined toward answering questions if asked, but without volunteering much beyond. Perhaps that had been the intention. Willie Camarel seemed drawn toward them as a group, maybe because of the image of solidarity and protection he saw in them. In return, his better schooling made him good to have around for help with the math and physics classes. He was from Oklahoma, Linc had learned, where his family ran a hard-sell Bible TV station. This was the only sure way Willie had been able to think of to escape.

"Do you have any particular plans on what you're going to do?" Willie asked.

"You mean in two days' time—when we get back in touch with the rest of that huge world out there?"

"Right."

Linc shrugged. "Wander around the station and check out what's happening, I guess. Maybe try the Low-g Court in the Axle. I hear it's fun. Got any better suggestions?"

"Not really. Mind if I tag along?"

"Not at all."

Willie glanced at Linc as they came to the lime-painted alloy stairs leading up to the billet deck. "Sometimes I kind of envy the way you guys had it," he said, as if an explanation were called for. "It's as if it equipped you to deal with anything, know what I mean? Maybe the rest of us missed out somehow."

Linc snorted. "You're crazy. You didn't miss anything. Believe me."

When they came to the billet, Rocky, who bunked above Linc, was engaged in his favorite occupation of stretching out and contemplating the ceiling. Flash was farther along the room, talking with Arvin. There were others scattered around, some grabbing a few minutes of reading, one playing solitaire, a couple attending to their kit. A big advantage of being in space was not having to clean up after hours of rolling around in sand and dirt and mud. Schultz was always looking for ways of making up for what must have been, to him, an intolerable deficiency.

Since distancing himself from Arvin, Flash had been taking on the role of a go-between, trying to stay on as good terms with Arvin as his solidarity with Linc permitted—maybe hoping to reconcile things between them. Linc didn't really have a problem with that, but as far as he was concerned he had nothing more to prove, and it was up to Arvin to make the moves. Although Arvin's star had dimmed a magnitude or two since their final run-in at Seville Trace, Linc wasn't entertaining high expectations. Arvin seemed to have retreated inward, keeping to himself far more than he had previously—no doubt due in part to his not having anyone to connive with when nobody stepped in to fill Welsh's place. Whatever the reason, Linc wasn't about to lose any sleep over the matter. It wasn't the biggest thing in his life. New times lay ahead, and the days were too busy.

"I was thinking," Rocky greeted Linc and Willie, looking down as they came in. "And no, it didn't hurt. Not so much that you'd notice, anyway."

"What?" Linc said.

"That Low-g Court they've got in the Axle. The pool in there is supposed to be quite something. I reckon we should go look at it."

"We were just talking about that. Willie says he'll be stringing along with us too."

"Great."

"How much room is there? Does anyone know?" Flash called over. "I mean, if we all hit it at once, is it gonna cram the place out? Maybe we should do it a bunch at a time and organize some kind of schedule."

"I don't think that'll be too much of a problem. By the sound of it, most of the guys'll be heading for the rec deck," Linc answered.

"Why? What's there?"

"What do you think? What planet are you just back from, Rocky?"

"Oh. Right."

Willie had squatted down to stow his gear back in his locker. "I hope you get to meet my uncle when we finally make the Zone, Flash," he said over his shoulder. "Did I ever tell you that he's into computers too? Now there's somebody whose brains you need to pick."

"You sorta mentioned it a couple of times," Flash said. "So what kinda stuff's he into?"

"Oh, it gets a bit technical. Control and sequencing systems mainly—involved with confinement fields and plasmas. From his mail I think it's connected with fusion: energy systems and propulsion."

Flash and Linc exchanged silent looks of bafflement. Sometimes Willie forgot they came from different worlds.

Linc realized that Arvin had been staring at him fixedly. It was there again—an unspoken intimation of something waiting to be said. Linc tried to act normally and show that he was approachable, yet without going out of his way to make things too easy either. There were rules. . . . And then once again, Arvin seemed to change his mind at the last instant and turned away to busy himself with something else. Before Linc was able to make anything more of it, the door opened and Senior Cadet Sulliman, Derek J., who was doing the clerking shift in the Day Office, appeared. Seniors were ones who had completed the initial two months and as such carried a single stripe on their sleeves. "Hey, Marani. You've got a phone call."

Linc looked at Rocky. They both raised their eyebrows. "Only one way to find out," Rocky said in answer to the unspoken obvious.

Cadets in the Turret lived in the Stone Age. Personal mobiles were not permitted, and the only communication was via a line in the Interview Room next to the Day Office, which they all had to share. Linc followed Sulliman back into the corridor and through some connecting passages to the Admin Section, where Sulliman gestured toward the door of the Interview Room and walked away. Linc let himself in, eased down into one of the seats at the fold-down metal table, and picked up the handset from its cradle.

"Linc Marani here."

"Is that the general, sir? Permission to speak, please?"

"Who is this?"

"You don't recognize me already? What are they feeding you guys in there? Or do you only recall on order now?"

The voice conjured up an image of red hair and a beefy face patchy with freckles. "Mace?" Linc grinned suddenly. "Is that you?"

"You took your time."

"It would have helped if you'd said so. Are you up here on Grayling now?"

"I sure am. In fact, we got here over a week ago. But people said not to overdo it on contacting you guys—not for the first four weeks, anywise."

"Yeah, that's the way it is. So did it all work out with the rigger number you were trying to land? You're all set?"

"It looks like it. There was just some extra stuff they wanted to put us through down at Yuc before we shipped up."

"That's terrific, Mace. We'll be coming out of here in another two days. You can tell me the whole score then. So who else is up here now?"

"Well, that's what I was really calling you about, Linc. Your old buddy Rick made it."

"*Say!* . . ."

"They told him he can be a carpenter."

Linc shook his head. "That's crazy. How many trees they got growing in the Zone?"

"Beats the hell outta me. . . . And Vic's here."

"Don't tell me. And he's gonna be a chef, right?"

"How'd you guess?" There was a short pause. Then, "Oh, yes. And I almost forgot. There's also someone that I thought you might be particularly interested in. Do you remember a certain number that was also at Coulie—black hair, eyes made outta ice, makes you think of a cat made out of velvet when she moves?"

Something like an electric jolt hit Linc in the back of the neck and traveled down to his shoes. He blinked. "You mean Julie?"

"Ah, right. That was her name. Seems she may have talents in a medical direction too, and right now she's working an orderly stint in the North Wing sick bay. I just happen to have her number here, if you think you'd maybe like to . . . you know, give her a call and say hi or something."

"You really think she'd be interested?" Just at the moment, Linc was having trouble collecting back together the mess of pieces that his thoughts had fragmented into. It was one of the rare moments when he realized he was saying something inane.

"Why not just call the number and find out?" Mace suggested.

CHAPTER TWENTY-FOUR

THE Recreation Deck was located near the bottom of the West Tower, along with two accommodation levels and a cluster of general-purpose compartments that served as meeting rooms, classrooms, and the like, as required. (Since centrifugal force increased and was directed away from the spin axis, the outward direction was "down," and the towers came together at their "tops.") The rec deck provided local catering in the West Tower and served as the general entertainment and social center for the whole station. In the latter capacity it boasted a bar of limited stock (age limit for alcohol, eighteen), tables and booths for seating, and a corner area available for dancing when it wasn't being used as a stage for theatrical, cabaret, or musical presentations. Adjoining space on the same level housed the general gym and a gallery with various games and amusements.

Linc arrived early from the conveyor elevator in which he'd traveled from the Axle. It was just a regular evening, with no special events scheduled. He had dropped out of the group that he had intended coming with originally, explaining that something had come up causing him to make other plans. He got himself a frail ale at the counter and moved to a far corner, where he selected one of the small, fold-down wall-tables with just two seats. Since space was at a premium everywhere in Grayling, a larger booth or a table would have been an invitation to share. He was hoping for a little of the nearest to privacy that could be hoped for.

The place was starting to fill up after being freed up from whatever it had been used for during the day. The music was piped—a mix of slow-and-easies and rock classics from the late nineteen hundreds to warm up the dancers. It would speed up later. Arvin was there already, sitting on the far side with one of the regular recruits and a couple of civilians—it was strange how naturally the word came to mind to describe the rest of the world already. Kamila, the Iraqi schoolteacher, was there with her husband. Liz was sitting with a couple at a table nearby, constantly looking toward the door—probably waiting for Rocky. Most of the other guys hadn't shown up yet.

Linc had tried calling Julie right away after talking to Mace, while he still had the phone, but she was working that shift. So he'd just left his number. She'd called back ten minutes before lights-out in the billet—Linc's second call in a few hours, provoking undisguised disapproval from Senior Cadet Sulliman. So there hadn't been time for them to say very much. But she had wanted to talk to him. He sensed it in her voice. She had learned from the others that he was there but been reluctant to bother him after what she'd heard about the first month of cadet training. (Or had there been a touch of the female not wishing to appear too eager? He was hardly going to run far.) She was doing okay, she'd told him, working hard but discovering new sides to herself. The same with him, Linc had told her. They'd arranged to meet in the rec deck when Linc and the other rookies got their leave.

He had saved a set of dress grays fresh from the laundry, taken extra care shaving and combing his hear after he showered, and used an aftershave, which he normally didn't bother with. He fiddled with his can and fidgeted, finding he was unable to maintain the relaxed cool that was normally his style.

"Hey, partner. Used to wear a uniform not too different myself. Old navy man. Is anybody using the seat?" Linc looked up. The speaker was in his fifties maybe, with lean, ruddy features and a crooked nose showing veins. Someone late in life to be starting anew, just wanting to talk. Linc forced a grin.

"Sorry, sir, but it's taken. I'd be happy to another time."

"It'd be my pleasure. Excuse me." The former sailor moved away.

Why, Linc asked himself, did he feel like some kid on a first date, anxious not to make a mess of it? Because, he supposed when he thought about it, he was a kid on a first real date with someone he didn't know too well, and he didn't want to make a mess of it. He shook his head to himself and sipped his drink.

"Hey, Linc, what's the matter? Scared we'll give you some kind of disease? Come on over." More cadets had arrived and were crowding around the bar counter.

"I've been living in a tin can long enough with you people," Linc threw back.

"Didn't you hear? Linc's deserted already. Big date tonight—a face from the past."

"Seriously?"

"Oh, big action, man. . . ."

"Is that right, Linc? She bringing any friends? Don't forget who your buddies are, now. Who helped you out with that R-13 today?"

"Hey," a different kind of voice said behind him. He turned back. Julie had come in while he was looking the other way. The expected medley of hoots and comments came from the gang but faded rapidly into the unheeded wastelands beyond the fringe of Linc's awareness.

She was wearing a simple, short-sleeved top with a dark skirt—the exact colors were lost in the light. Her eyes shone their silent, mischievous laughter, even here. He had forgotten the lines of the firm mouth set in the tapered face. She had her hair shorter than at Coulie. Linc stood up awkwardly—something he'd never done for a girl before. A little of Dr. Grober coming back, maybe. Guys who had style did it in movies. For some reason all of a sudden, none of the lines he had rehearsed in his head felt right. "Hi," he managed instead.

Julie looked him over approvingly. "My, I like the outfit!"

"Oh, really?"

"It's very . . . There's a word, but I can't think of it." They both smiled together, self-consciously. Linc realized that she had been as nervous as he. She sat down.

"Can I get you something from the bar?" Linc said.

Julie motioned toward the can on the table. "One of those would be fine. Maybe something to munch on too."

"Sure. . . . Er, I'll be right back."

He returned a couple of minutes later with her drink and a bowl of mixed snacks, and sat with his back turned solidly toward the smirks and looks being directed across the room. The dancing was picking up in the open square nearby, which made the room seem bigger and generated a better feeling of privacy. Julie had put on a perfume that smelled good, Linc noticed.

They made halting small talk for a while, exchanging bits of news on others they had both known at Coulie. Julie hadn't heard further of Angelo, which surprised both of them since he had seemed likely to go far. Shel had gone to Boston but been RPO'd there, and Karen had quit too rather than carry on without her. Insecurities eased gradually, and talk became more relaxed. Julie had decided, after a few stints of helping out in the sick bay, that nursing was what she wanted. For the first time, Linc was able to ask her about the background that had resulted in her ending up at Coulie.

"Oh . . ." Julie looked away, as if for a pointer to where to begin. "It was one of those stories of not being exactly the luckiest person in the world parentwise, you know. . . ."

"In what kind of way?" Linc asked.

"You've probably heard it all before—the drugs-and-drink scene."

Linc nodded.

"I mean, big. Somebody got the police to break in when I'd been left on my own for two days—I'm talking about way back, when I was just a baby. I got taken away, and after that it was care centers, then finally a foster family. That was all in L.A., where I grew up."

"And that didn't work out?" Linc guessed from her tone.

Julie shook her head. "It was horrible. They had three kids of their own, but there was this double standard—as if I was the house servant or something. There were a lot of books there, but I was the only one who read them. I think that made the parents kinda mad too, as if their kids were stupid. . . . Well, they *were* stupid. They could have had anything."

"So, what happened?"

Julie selected a cashew nut from the snack food and sighed. "Oh . . . I took off finally and got in with the bad side—people with expensive habits, who cleaned high-end pads to pay for them. I never did much stuff, but I ran wheels. Somebody snitched, and I got stopped hauling a load to a fence in Sherman Oaks."

"One-timer? A file sheet like yours and you got sent down?" Linc made a dubious face.

"There was this cop in the Junior Services Division. He thought he had me set up. The case background was perfect. But I said I wouldn't play, and they could do what they liked." Julie shrugged. "So I get a ticket for the main line, but then at the last minute another option comes up. . . . And the rest you know." She sent across a questioning look. Linc knew the routine. Female favors demanded; if not granted, somebody would be sure to find drugs and implications to other unsolved things. His anger probably showed, but he made no more of it. "How about you?" Julie asked.

Linc summarized his own story as it was—plain and straight, without trying to embellish or excuse anything. Julie watched his face intently while she listened. It was one of the few times Linc had ever had the feeling of somebody taking an interest in him just for his own sake. He was unaccustomed to it. People had only shown an interest in him for what they thought they could get.

"I take it you're done with all that now," she said when he had finished.

"Well, there are a couple of scores I still have to settle. Then I'll be done with it."

Julie looked at him doubtfully, then seemed to decide that she didn't want to pursue the subject. Instead, her gaze strayed back to his uniform. "I was surprised when they told me you'd gone in for the military," she said. "It didn't sound like you somehow. You seem, oh, I don't know . . . like the kind of person who could do without people pushing him around."

"It wasn't what I wanted," Linc said. "I was more interested in engineering—making and shaping things. But I guess that sometimes we're not as smart as we think. I couldn't get the hang of the math part of it."

"That's funny. I never thought of you as doing some kind of job in a factory either."

Linc waved a hand. "That wasn't what I meant. It was more, you know—creating mechanisms, precision parts."

"You mean like the guys who made guns and things in the old movies?"

"More than that. The prototypes of instruments and machines, the things you see inside turbines and engines. . . . There's something about being able to make parts accurate to a tenth of a thousandth of an inch, and then fit them together into something that works. It's like an art. You feel as if—"

"Yes, it is!" A grinning black figure with curly hair came around the knot of dancers. "Hey, Linc! How's it all been?"

"Rick, old buddy! Just fine. I heard you were up here too."

"How come?"

"Mace called the other day. He told me."

"Say, that's right." Rick looked at Julie. "You didn't waste much time nailing him."

"Mace had a hand in it," Julie said.

"Sounds nice and sociable of him."

"So what's all this about you're gonna be a carpenter of all things?" Linc said to Rick. "How much carpentering d'you expect to find out there? You think they're gonna start growing trees on asteroids or something?"

"It's all different there. Wood is like a precious metal. Think of luxury ornaments and special decorations. . . ."

Rick trailed off and looked away as the sound of voices rising came from farther along the room. Three young men, in their late teens or early twenties, were standing over a table where Willie Camarel and another cadet were sitting with two girls. "No, I don't want to! I'm sitting here talking," one of the girls shouted, shaking a hand off her arm.

The one standing between the other two, who looked like the leader, was heavily built and holding a half-full plastic beaker. His eyes were puffy and his expression mean. "What's the matter? You think these fancy clothes make 'em better 'n us or something?" His voice grew to a bellow. "I mean, doesn't everyone know that half of 'em are trash that the jails wouldn't take? Ain't that right, boy?" He jabbed Willie on the shoulder. "You think that makes you a soldier? Figure you could take me on, huh?" The dancers were stopping and looking across. The music cut.

"Look, I really don't want any trouble," Willie pleaded.

The youth tipped part of his drink over Willie's jacket. "Is that so? Well, that's good, 'cause I just had an accident."

"Excuse me," Linc said, slipping out from his seat.

"Linc . . ." Julie called after him. But it was just a token gesture.

He got there at the same moment as Arvin from the opposite direction. "Okay, guys, why don't we just cool it. . . ." Linc began. But then three of the veteran troops cut in. One was Dierot, a former Israeli tank man and French *para* who had fought seemingly everywhere, was as hard as tool steel and looked it; the way the other two moved in was equally deterring.

"*Break it up!*" Dierot barked. "We're all 'ere to 'ave a good time, okay? Some other nice girls will dance with you later. You guys just go take a little walk around the gallery. Get yourselves some coffee." The leader of the three youths backed off sullenly. They let themselves be herded away by the soldiers.

"Are you okay, Willie?" Linc asked.

"Sure, it's over. Thanks anyhow," Willie said, dabbing his jacket with a napkin.

There was nothing more for Linc and Arvin to do. Flash, who had also appeared from somewhere, came up behind them. Music started up again, and the deejay's voice came over the speaker system. "Okay, folks, the excitement's over. That's it. Let's get moving again with something from way back in the nineteen seventies. . . ."

Flash looked from Linc to Arvin and gestured at them appealingly. "See, guys," he said. "We're all on the same side, right? We're all going out there together. Wouldn't this be a good time for you two to just shake and get rid of this thing that's been going on too long around here?"

It seemed a good time to Linc. He shrugged, nodded, and put out a hand. Arvin stared at it, seemed to want to, then shrank back. "I can't," he muttered, turning away stiffly, and went back to his table.

"There has to be—" Flash began, but Linc cut him off.

"I'm the wrong guy, Flash. Go talk to him. I've got company waiting."

Although Linc remained moody for a while longer, he gradually got over it. Rick stayed with him and Julie, and the conversation picked up to more cheerful things. Julie eventually got Linc up onto the dance floor, and it was only then that he learned her full name for the first time. It was Yeats; Julie Yeats. Willie and his three friends got them to move to their table, everyone got a chance to dance with everyone, and the evening ended on a party note all around.

Afterward, Linc accompanied Julie back to her quarters in the East Tower. She clung to his arm and stayed close on the way to a boarding point for the moving-belt elevator, during the ascent to the Axle, and through the descent back down the other tower. She shared a cabin there with three other females, but the approach section was like part of the interior of a battleship superstructure, with compartments, stairwells, and cubbyholes enough for anyone who wanted privacy. But Linc settled for a hug and a kiss after walking her to her door. The fragrance and the feel of her nearness for a few seconds were enough. And he sensed gratitude and elation in her response—that he understood and respected how she felt.

He felt good all the way back through the Axle again and on up to the Turret. Some of the other guys might hoot derisively—because they would ask, and he would tell them. Let them, he decided. It was one of the few times in life when something inside told him unequivocally that he had done the right thing. He wasn't used to feeling that about himself. Sergeant Schultz would have been proud.

CHAPTER TWENTY-FIVE

IT was the first time since coming up to Grayling that Linc was without the feeling of solid walls enclosing him. *Above* and *below* had lost their meanings. All around him in every direction, stars shone with the brilliance that had awed him when he stared out at them on the first day of his arrival. Even Grayling Station was reduced to no more than a distorted cruciform ten miles away, the sunlight picking out different surfaces and glinting off the moving lines as it turned. To one side, the half Moon hung white against the blackness, looking six times its size from Earth. Less then a mile away, almost in line with Grayling, was the outstation known as the Construction Shack, a one-hundred-foot-diameter sphere buried in a clutter of tanks, cylinders, and boxlike protuberances that gave the impression more of having sprouted haphazardly than of being a product of design. Other, smaller structures and clumps of latticework floated not far off, with movements of jet-suited figures and assorted vehicles operating around them discernible in the vicinity. This was where the new recruits—military and civilian technicians alike—came to learn the basics of space construction. The theoretical introductions were over now; it was time to begin learning the skills that would be needed for what lay ahead.

"Enough stargazing, Marani." Lieutenant Koln's voice sounded in Linc's helmet—Koln had a screen that monitored Linc's view field. "Let's get back to some work here."

"Just resting my eyes."

Linc returned his gaze to the task at hand. It involved attaching a tank and pump to a frame assembly floating in space, and then installing the connecting pipework and hoses. The manipulators that Linc was controlling had five fingers and were jointed to mimic the motions of a human hand. "Sys on. View schematic, page three," he said aloud. A diagram showing part of the system he was building appeared in his field of vision. "Detail G7." A valve and its surroundings enlarged. "Rotate Z-minus, thirty. . . . Rotate X-plus, ten." Linc studied the arrangement for a few seconds. "Sys off." The schematic vanished. Linc positioned a next length of pipe and commenced making the joint.

"Take your time. You're doing just fine," Lieutenant Koln said.

A mile or so off to Linc's left, in front of the distant green jewel of Jade, a skeleton of girders and lattices the size of a city block hung like an engineer's drawing printed on the starry backdrop. Christened Hermes, it would eventually become a transfer station placed in a highly elliptical orbit to cycle permanently between intercepts with the orbits of Mars and Earth. The Outzoners figured that besides its usefulness to themselves, such a facility would offer services that could be traded for many needs they would depend on Earth to supply for a while longer yet. The concept of a cycling station had been around for many years, but projected times for building it had always fallen outside the ten-year "window of feasibility" that had plagued Earth-bound administrations. Projects not completed during that time were almost inevitably defunded or canceled by new political regimes with different aims and priorities. Hence, few truly ambitious schemes had a believable chance of ever becoming reality.

Grayling Station had been part of an original plan to develop a broad-based space manufacturing and construction capability using materials sent up from the Moon. That program had never become much more than artist's impressions in glossy PR brochures for stockholders, and worsening political complications made the prospects for further large-scale commitment uncertain at best.

At least that was so in the near-Earth regions of space. To avoid interference, the Outzoners obtained and processed the bulk of their materials distantly—which, in any case, was where they were used. Hence, Grayling was a relic of an idea that had come and then foundered, rather than the beginnings of anything expected to grow significantly.

Large-scale construction in space was comparatively easy. On Earth there was gravity to contend with. Most of the design difficulties with large structures stemmed from having to devise ways of getting them to stand under their own weight. Assembly involved balancing and swinging large beams into position and then supporting them while they were fixed with welds, fasteners, rivets, or the like. In space there was no weight. Low-mass assemblies sufficed and could be gently floated into place and secured without the hazards of collapse or injury from accidental falls. And since much of the assembly process was repetitive, consisting of attaching the same basic forms over and over again, it could be performed by robots. Linc quite enjoyed being out where the yellow-painted robots crawled along the extending structures, guiding them with laser designators to indicate where and how the next unit was to be positioned. In a way it was creating artistry in metal of a different kind. . . . However, today he was doing tanks and pipes.

He finished the last joint, pressured up the system as directed, and verified from a sixty-second sampling of the gauges that there were no major leaks. He called down the log sheet, checked the items he had completed, and Koln signed them off as inspected and passed. "Okay, you can take a break, Marani. That was good. Camarel, let's see you try the next section."

Linc exited from the system, took off the VR helmet he had been wearing, and was instantly back at a console inside the Construction Shack, a mile from the remote-directed "waldo" assembly robot he'd been controlling. He took off the wired gloves and unsnapped the restraint holding him in his "seat." Willie floated in to take his place and prepared to run the initiation drill. Flash and Arch were at other consoles nearby, also in helmets, the screens above them showing respectively a close-up of manipulators connecting power cables to a terminal box, and a reference chart from the library back at Grayling. Senior Cadet Ross, the fifth member of the team with Koln that day, was standing by, ready to assist.

Koln moved to look at Flash's monitor. "Make sure to use the sticky prod to pick up those metal clippings. They aren't going to fall out of the way anywhere. If there's one place they can short something out, they'll find it."

"Will do, sir," Flash's voice acknowledged from a speaker grille.

Koln moved his gaze to Arch's screen. "Are you still awake in there, Egan? We've had this instruction sheet up here for the last five minutes."

"I'm trying to remember how to reprogram from spot weld to seam," Arch answered.

"Okay, what you need to do is go back up another level to get the function macros. . . ."

Construction was a good way of attaining general, all-round extravehicular-activity capability. EVA would become as much a part of life out in space as using sidewalks or crossing the street in a city. In addition, for the military, familiarity with structures would be a necessary preliminary to later learning the arts of close-in space assault tactics, entering and securing, disabling and demolition, and so forth.

Larger screens on the rear wall showed views in different directions around the shack. In the distance beyond Grayling, appearing as a foreshortened finger of silver viewed almost end-on, was the long-range transporter ship *Constellation* that had arrived from the Outzone in the last few days and would be returning there shortly. Many of the transients passing through Grayling would be departing with it, with a new intake from Earth coming up to take their place. Those who had made senior cadet would be moving on. Mace would be going on an accelerated plan, since space riggers were urgently needed out there. And Rick would be going—there was nothing for him to practice his future occupation on at Grayling. The professions evidently took precedence over rank-and-file military. Linc and the others could only hope their turn would come next time.

"It takes you a minute or two to adjust to being back inside, doesn't it?" Ross said to Linc. Koln was still talking to Arch.

"Right," Linc agreed. In operation a waldo anchored itself to the structure it was working on. After you got used to the feeling of immovability that came from controlling it and sensing through it, coming out of the link again into zero-gravity surroundings made you reel all over the place.

"You in for the poker game tonight?"

Linc shook his head. "Passing again this time."

"Okay, don't tell me."

Linc sent him a what-else-can-I-tell-you? shrug and looked back at the screens showing the panoramas outside. Now that the month of accelerated basics was over, life for the cadets had eased somewhat. They were assigned to other officers for spells, instead of being captives of Schultz all the time—although, now, looking back, Linc found he couldn't view Schultz other than with what could only be described as a kind of affection. Leave breaks were given regularly, which meant being able to see Julie when their schedules permitted. And that fact alone had made a big difference in his existence. For the first time he had the feeling something clean and decent had come into his life, something he didn't want to risk spoiling.

Yes, indeed, Linc reflected as he gazed out at the universe. For once, things seemed to be taking on a definitely more pleasant aspect.

CHAPTER TWENTY-SIX

THROUGH the days that followed, shuttles arrived from various parts of Earth, bringing more who would be joining the *Constellation*. Accommodation aboard the ship was not always ready on time, and Grayling Station became a staging post, filled beyond its normal capacity. There were so many comings and goings, people crowded into makeshift dormitories for a night and gone the next, vessels docking and leaving at the Axle, that there was little opportunity to check for names and faces that one might know. But chance encounters did occur among those who had been in earlier preparatory courses together.

Linc and Julie had grabbed the chance to unwind for an hour in the low-gravity exercise and pool area in the Axle. Rocky and Liz were with them, making the best of the unusual circumstance of all four getting a midday break together. They were sitting in a terrace area overlooking the Axle canteen, where the glass enclosing walls let them follow the docking operations at the ports outside and shuttles maneuvering around the *Constellation* in the distance. Below the terrace and the observation windows ran a gallery carrying a traffic of people moving between the docking ports and other parts of Grayling.

"Oh, I got hauled in through getting mixed up in what my older brother was into," Rocky told the others. "He used to be with the Canadian counterterrorism units and kinda ended up running his own private army when he got out. You know, stashing illegal weapons—they're real hot on that up there. Paramilitary things with other vets."

"What kind of things?" Julie asked.

"Oh . . . contract services for people who maybe wanted to exert a little pressure somewhere, you know—like dealers being slow on payment. Or maybe who are worried about protecting assets they'd rather the government didn't know about. Anyway, when they got me it was over some trumped-up thing because they figured I'd be able to give them names. So I ended up with these four guys in a back room for, you know, the treatment—and they must have been there for practice or something because they weren't much more than kids themselves. Well, I creamed all four of 'em pretty good, and they didn't like that at all. . . ." Rocky paused while Liz emitted a peal of delighted laughter. She had no doubt heard it before but apparently never tired of it. "And that put me in the line for a deep hole somewhere, except that this option came up." Rocky shrugged and gestured around. "And here I am."

"Well, I'm sure glad it did," Liz said, clasping his arm.

"Did your brother show you how to fight too?" Linc asked.

Rocky nodded. "Oh sure. He learned it with the military. Used to fight as an army boxer too. You wouldn't want to mess with him."

"Where is he now?" Julie asked.

"I'm not sure. Life got too cramped, so he moved on.

Down south somewhere, I heard—South America. There's action there. That'd be enough."

Linc got the feeling that Rocky probably knew more. There were ways people like that stayed in touch. And good reasons why they kept it to themselves.

"Hey, get a load of that one moving in toward the *Constellation* now," Liz said, nodding toward the window wall. "Aren't those Russian markings on it?"

The others turned their heads to look. "Heavy freight lifter," Rocky pronounced. "They boost them up with ground lasers. Maybe it's full of wood to panel some general's bedroom."

"That would keep Rick busy for a while," Julie said.

Linc looked away. The table they were sitting at was by a rail looking down one of the stairways to the gallery. Among the figures moving in slow bounds or by pulling along the handrails below were three men together, one of them in a tan uniform that caught his eye—similar to the kind worn by the coaches at Coulie. One of the other two was in a regular casual jacket, while the third, in the center, carrying a briefcase, wore the black suit and reversed collar of a cleric. Linc sat up sharply as they came nearer and the light caught the priest's features. He was of dark, Mexican appearance with a thin mustache. Linc tugged Julie's sleeve and nodded. "Tell me I'm not seeing things. Is that guy in the middle down there Angelo from Coulie, or is it Angelo from Coulie?"

Julie leaned across the table to see and then gasped. "Oh, my God!" she exclaimed. "It is! . . . But what's he doing in that outfit?"

"Who's Angelo?" Rocky asked.

"Somebody we were with in Phase One. Linc's first real friend there," Julie replied.

"I'll be right back," Linc said, getting up.

He loped across to the stairs and descended as fast as was possible in the reduced gravity, floating like a balloon on his feet and moving more by pulling with his hands. By the time he caught up with the group, they had turned a corner into the main corridor leading to the docking ports and unloading bays. "Hey, Angelo!" he called. The figure in the dark suit stopped and looked back. Then his face split into the familiar wide grin.

"Linc!" The two men with Angelo looked at him questioningly. He said something to them. They nodded and moved on.

"Don't forget the gate closes in fifteen minutes," one of them called back.

Linc and Angelo moved to one side of the corridor, out of the flow of people, and shook hands warmly. Linc spread his arms in disbelief. "I thought you'd have lost that tan out here" was all he could think of to say just at that moment.

"Why? The Sun's stronger. So how you been making out? Doing okay?"

"Sure. We went through Seville T., in Texas."

"Uh-huh." Angelo nodded. It evidently needed no explaining. "You're looking great. The military, eh? Somehow I wouldn't have thought it."

"Oh, I didn't exactly plan things that way, but that's another story. How about you? Where did you go from Coulie?"

"Oh, a little here, a little there. You know how they move you around."

"Right. Always hectic. Say, you remember Julie?"

"Julie with the eyes? Who wouldn't?"

"She's here too—in fact, with some friends just a little way back there. Do you want to stop by?"

Angelo showed his palms. "I'd love to, but I'm boarding in a few minutes. Shipping back out with the *Constellation.* You say hi to her for me, you hear? Tell her we'll all meet up again in the Zone sometime. And that's a promise."

"Oh, too bad. So you'll actually be on your way out there tomorrow? . . ." Linc's brow creased. Did Angelo just say shipping *back* out? He stared again at Angelo's clothes, the unvoiced question written across his face. Angelo had evaded saying exactly what he'd done after Coulie. Certainly, nothing about going on to a Phase Two anywhere. Angelo returned an easy grin and waited, letting Linc figure out the implication for himself.

And then it hit him. "You were right," Linc breathed, staring incredulously. "That first time we met, when I was digging that ditch after Royal whined out. There *were* plants in Coulie. *You* were one of them!"

Angelo looked apologetic but kept smiling. "Hey, it was the only way, you know. We had to be aware of what was happening among you guys. Somebody had to be in there to start breaking down all that distrust and anger, and begin turning it around. And, I mean, getting dragged up rock faces and having to help you deal with situations like Arvin. . . ."

"He's a cadet here too," Linc said, still in a dazed voice.

"There are easier ways of making a living, you know, man. No hard feelings, eh?"

It was true. Angelo had been the first person to treat Linc with anything like decency, that day. It was Angelo who had insisted on their going back to the counter to compliment the kitchen girl's efforts. Angelo had been the first to stand next to Linc when he'd faced Arvin and the other two alone. . . .

"It's okay," Linc said, although he hadn't fully absorbed it. "Back then I might have gotten mad. But now I've seen too much."

Angelo seemed relieved and genuinely pleased. "You'll do okay now. Believe me. I've seen a lot. One of the reasons they picked me is that I'm older than you probably think."

"So you're actually going back. . . ." Angelo's nod told Linc there was no need to complete the question. "Is it really everything they say out there?" Linc asked instead.

"More than they say. It's not so much the luxuries—forget all that. But being among people who are alive, who haven't had the spirit drained out of them. You'll see it for yourself. Another ship's due out next month—the *Neil A. Armstrong*. I'll lay a dollar to a cent you'll be on it."

"You really think so?"

"We need everyone we can get. . . ." Angelo glanced at his watch. "Well . . ."

"I'll run into you again out there, maybe."

"You bet. I'll make a point of tracking you down."

"Then, take care, okay. . . . And thanks, really—for everything."

"Just doing my job." Angelo began moving away.

"I never even told you who I am," Linc called after him.

Angelo looked back from among other figures going the same way. "It's okay, I know. Linc Marani, right?"

Linc stood watching him recede, until suddenly the rest dawned on him. "I don't know yours," he shouted out.

"Hilvarez," Angelo's voice carried back.

CHAPTER TWENTY-SEVEN

THE mothballing of the program to build space constructions using lunar material had left substantial quantities of orbiting moon rock that had never been used. The Outzoners had consolidated much of this into a single mass they christened *Sisyphus*—essentially an artificial subsatellite of the Moon, equipped for deploying tether lines out into space that could be extended for several hundreds of miles. The object was to use *Sisyphus* as an orbital flywheel to store temporarily the excess momentum shed by vessels slowing down on arrival from the outer solar system. It could then be transferred back when they departed.

Instead of expending enormous amounts of energy to brake itself down to the velocity of the Earth-Moon system about the Sun, the *Constellation* had attached to a tether from *Sisyphus* and performed a complex, end-about-end maneuver around the Moon, from which it emerged on a rendezvous orbit that could easily be matched to Grayling's, while *Sisyphus* was boosted to a higher lunar orbit. When the time came for the *Constellation* to be launched back out, the process would be reversed, leaving *Sisyphus* back as it started (or close, anyway—some thrust would be needed to make good the inevitable losses). An enthusiastic orbital-dynamics engineer had come into one of the classrooms to describe the operation to the cadets, but Linc didn't really get the hang of it until Willie explained it again later. It sounded like a cool idea. *Sisyphus* took its name from a king in Greek mythology who was condemned to spend eternity rolling a heavy rock to the top of a mountain, upon which it always rolled down again.

In the final hours before launch, Grayling Station grew quiet after the noise and bustle that had become normal over the previous few days, its population down to half or less of its normal complement. There would be cleaning and general tidying to do in preparation for the new arrivals after the *Constellation* departed, but in the meantime the cadets who were staying were put on light duties. Linc found himself with a group that included Rocky, Flash, and Willie in the garrison messroom inside the Turret, where operations around the *Constellation* were being shown on the large screen at one end of the room. Most of the regular troops had moved out as well as the senior cadets, and the mess was also unusually quiet and missing faces that had become familiar.

The view coming in at present was from a support craft standing several miles off from the ship. *Constellation* had a mass of the order of that of a large naval carrier but was larger, being of much lighter construction. The clutter of supplies and equipment that had floated about it had gradually been absorbed inside over the last days. Now the last ferries had detached and the service vessels pulled back to leave it hanging alone against the background of stars, an immense, white-and-gray elongation of hull forms, superstructures, and holding tanks, held together by frameworks and structural booms. From the cluster of spheres housing the passenger quarters and command deck in the nose, to the final stages of the drive system behind radiation shielding at the stern, it measured just over a mile.

Linc had mixed feelings as he stared at it. On the one hand he was awed, on the other, puzzled. If humans could produce something as stunning as this and solve all the problems it symbolized, why couldn't they get their act together to create a world that worked? Would the Outzoners finally achieve it in their attempt to discard the old values and start anew? Or would that experiment too, eventually, end up the same way as all the others seemed to have done?

"Eight minutes and thirty seconds to burn, and counting." The voice of one of the controllers in Grayling's Bridge came over the audio. *"The hook is deployed and on target."* This meant that *Sisyphus* was coming around the Moon in its higher orbit, swinging down its line like a three-hundred-mile grapnel. Linc thought about Mace and Rick out there at this very moment; Kamila, the Iraqi teacher, and her husband; all the others, how they must be feeling. Angelo was there too, but this wasn't his first time. Linc thought back to those who had quit or been sent back, and felt glad, more than ever before, that he was not among them. He wanted to be looking forward to a future now. The thought of having to go back to everything that had been the past would have been unbearable.

"Seven minutes."

"All systems green-go at seven-zero," another voice cut in. The view on the screen changed to a telescopic shot from somewhere showing the five-cluster of the *Constellation*'s massive drive nozzles in close-up. Their very quiescence now seemed somehow to emphasize the stupendous power dormant within, waiting to be unleashed. The ship would lift itself up to a matching trajectory before attaching to the tether for the extra boost that would slingshot it out and away. Afterward, it would continue under powered acceleration for an additional thirty hours, achieving a velocity at the end of that time that would carry it to the vicinity of Jupiter in just under a month. Six months ago Linc hadn't even been aware of such concepts. Now he devoured them and couldn't wait to be a part of what it all pointed to. The others around him seemed to be affected the same way. Rocky, stretched out and tilting back his chair to get as close to his favorite horizontal position as he could without tipping over, hadn't said a word for over ten minutes.

The view switched to another angle on the *Constellation*, this time showing a slender line, bright against the blackness, curving outward into space from a point somewhere close to amidships. The Moon was showing full to one side in the background. "That's the grab line that'll catch the tether," Willie said, gesturing. "It keeps the action away from the ship—in case there's a screwup."

"How thick are those lines?" Flash asked curiously.

"Under a centimeter of Carbosyn-20. Diamond fiber. Isn't it amazing how it catches the sunlight! The convexity acts as a magnifier."

Willie knew all the details, of course. Linc liked having him around, but there were times when he could have done without the commentaries.

"Man, what would you give to be sitting out there with those guys now, waiting for it to fire," one of the other cadets drawled from somewhere behind.

"If Sulliman's there and I'm not, I'm happy to wait for the next one," another voice answered.

"Right on," somebody agreed.

"With our luck, the next one will have Schultz."

"No way. He'll be getting ready for the next batch of fresh fish here."

"Who do you figure will pick up the Clerical Two slot?" Rocky asked, coming out of his trance. An easy, laid-back job that Rocky couldn't miss being interested in.

"My money says Ilkes," someone offered.

"Just so long as it's not Arvin. . . . Where is Arvin? Anyone know?"

"I think he got stuck with janks," Willie said—cadet slang for janitorial duties around the Turret.

"*Five minutes and counting,*" the controller's voice announced. "*At the five-zero checkpoint we have plasma and fields within spec, go-green on all, and the hook is in the window. Confirmation to proceed has been issued.*" The numeric superposed at the top of the screen was already showing 04:53.

Linc wondered if Julie had managed to get time to watch the launch from the North Tower—she was working that day. Very likely, she would. It wasn't the kind of thing anyone would want to miss, and supervisors were generally cooperative. As a nursing student she could have taken a slot to go with the *Constellation* like Mace and Rick, but had opted to stay back and take a specialist class on dislocations and fractures in order to fly on the same ship as Linc later. They spent practically all their off-duty time together. The idea of one leaving for the Outzone without the other would have been unthinkable to either of them.

Flash regarded the image of the Moon for a while, obscuring the Earth beyond, his head cocked to one side in thought. "Do you know, it just occurred to me," he said, looking around. "Do you think the Zoners picked this spot deliberately—here, behind the Moon—to make it harder for Earth to follow the kinds of things they're up to? I mean, that ship looks pretty snazzy to me, compared to anything much else that I can remember seeing. Maybe they don't want people on Earth watching everything that's been going on. I bet a lot more's happening here at Grayling than most of them realize."

"From some of the things my uncle's said, there could be a lot more happening out in the Zone too," Willie said. "It might turn out that you ain't seen nothin' yet." Somebody whistled.

"*Three minutes, and counting. . . .*"

The screen switched to an internal view of the Grayling Bridge from where the operation was being coordinated, just three levels below the garrison. The crew stations and monitor panels were all manned, with the station director, Kelsoe, at the supervisory panel, looking tense, flanked by his executive officer and the chief engineering officer. Kelsoe was something of a godlike figure who led a remote existence somehow despite the confines of the place, and whom few of the cadets had actually seen in the flesh. Linc didn't envy the responsibilities he carried just at this moment. Once again, here was a whole area of human affairs that six months ago Linc would have had no concept of.

"I heard it from Ross that there's a permanent laser-communications link from the Zone right into there," Flash said, keeping his eyes on the screen. "The stuff on it's not for general distribution."

"Encrypted against Earth intercepts," Willie said.

"Something like that."

"Do you think they really could have deployed X-ray laser cannon, Camarel?" somebody asked.

Willie pursed his lips. "It's possible," he answered non-committally.

"How would you fancy having to take on one of those from a thousand miles off?" Flash said to Linc.

"I'd rather be out there in the Zone, sitting behind it," Linc told him.

The screen showed the view relayed from the tether winch installation on *Sisyphus*—the terminal pylon anchored on massive steel legs splaying out into the rock, the line arcing away and out of sight to lose itself somewhere in the direction of the Moon. Showing to one side beyond the Moon was a part of Earth.

"Diamond fiber, eh?" somebody murmured. "Just imagine, hundreds of miles of it."

"It wouldn't do you any good," Willie said. "In the Zone it has purely engineering value only."

Maybe Rick would end up as some kind of jeweler, Linc thought to himself. Wooden rings and necklaces. Now wouldn't that be something different.

"*Two minutes. . . .*"

"How's Liz doing?" Flash asked Rocky. He didn't really care just at that moment. It was a way of voicing out the tension rising in all of them.

"Okay. The office girls are having a postlaunch elbow-room party—to celebrate being able to breathe again. Eighteen hundred hours today in the rec deck."

"Great!"

"You gonna bring Julie, Linc? We need her there, man. One of the best dancers."

"I don't know yet. I need to check."

"What makes you think you'd get a turn anyway, Derkin? You know what those two are like."

"Aw, Linc's okay. Anyhow, gotta take a breather sometime. Right, Linc?"

"Hey, that depends on her and your own natural charm. We're not talking a property-rights thing here. Know what I mean?"

"Will that friend of Liz's be there?" Flash asked Rocky. "You know, the little blond one."

"You mean Pam? Oh, sure, she'll be there."

"That's it, then. I'm telling ya, I'm going for that one this time."

"No chance," one of the voices at the back opined.

"Watch me."

"You wouldn't enjoy her, even if you did try for her, Flash," another said.

"Oh, really? And how would you know?"

"I didn't."

"Get outta here, turkey. When were you ever closer than making eyes?"

"*One minute to burn. Deployment is good. Sequence set to slave on auto.*" The views on the screen changed to show in rapid succession an external shot of Grayling, the inside of the Bridge again, and then back to the *Constellation.* Other voices came onto the circuit:

"Plasma primaries are at heat, and go."

"Injection fields are go."

"Attitude and profile check positive function."

A cut back to the Bridge, with Kelsoe nodding to the CEO.

"*We have go at zero minus forty seconds. Drive initialization syncing now.*"

Conversation around the messroom had ceased. The figures lounging in the chairs and propped at the table became still. For some reason Linc had imagined these final seconds would tick by with an almost painful slowness, as if the world had gone into some kind of slow motion; but before he had even realized it, they were inside the last ten. The readout showed:

00:03 . . . 00:02 . . . 00:01 . . .

A pillar of light several times the length of the ship lanced out across space—blue at the head, turning through white and then yellow toward the tip.

"Injection. . . . Plasma ignition. . . . Acceleration registering. . . . We have liftout!"

Almost imperceptibly at first, the *Constellation* began moving against the background. Probably due to some trick of perspective as the angle changed, its nose seemed to lift, as if already straining to throw off the last restraints of gravity and find freedom in its natural element among the stars. The column of star fire extended. Already the ship was moving smoothly, now visibly foreshortening as its speed and distance increased. Linc's mind went out to those inside: engineers, clerks, teachers, soldiers, families with children, lonesome adventurers; some he had known, others he would maybe one day meet—all leaving everything they had known or might have been to seek some new, unknown destiny somewhere that most of them could never imagine. In a way he had never pictured before, he saw them as forerunners of the whole human race, bursting out from the mottled blue egg that had spawned it. And, goddamn it, he felt his eyes getting moist, and he couldn't control it. A tear welled out and ran down his cheek. He brushed it away hurriedly.

This was what he had come up here to be a part of. Perhaps something inside him had hungered for the things he was feeling now, all along. Linc didn't really understand how, but Willie said all life had evolved from fishes. Linc would no more be able to go back to his former life, he realized, than he could grow scales and return to the depths of the sea.

CHAPTER TWENTY-EIGHT

LINC completed his basic course under Schultz and received his senior's stripe. Almost certainly, that meant he would be going on the next ship out—confirmed as the *Neil A. Armstrong*, which Angelo had mentioned. And it could be quite soon, since more vessels were being completed and commissioned in the Zone, and traffic was expected to increase dramatically. Offsetting Linc's excitement to some degree was the news that he was considered to have officer potential but on arrival would be consigned to a preliminary two-year term as infantry marine—the "grunts" of the Outzone space forces. In the meantime he was posted to E Company, Construction, commanded by a Captain Ullerman.

Hermes, the transfer station being built to cycle between

the orbits of Mars and Earth, would probably be the last large-scale project the Outzoners would undertake in the near-Earth region of space—at least until Earth underwent some kind of radical political and economic change. The only factor likely to result in a decision to commence another local project would be its training value for future migrants on their way out, in the same manner as Hermes was being used as a training project for large-scale space construction.

Many parts of Hermes, such as the accommodation modules, plant and storage-tank housings, required shell forms of various kinds. These were assembled from sections tens or hundreds of feet across, produced in space by depositing metal-alloy vapor on inflated plastic balloon formers of the correct shapes. Deposition was carried out by remote-controlled, jet-guided robots that traversed back and forth, round and round, adding microlayer upon layer to the growing surfaces. They were called spiders on account of both the slender feelers they extended around the working area to position themselves, and the bulbous, abdomenlike reservoirs in which they melted and vaporized the metals to be deposited.

One of Linc's duties as senior cadet in his closing spell at Grayling was accompanying rookies who were still going through second-part basic on their first cautious space walks and ventures outside. Already he had graduated to the role of teacher. The basics of shell deposition was among the newly acquired arts that he found himself passing on to the newcomers.

The shell being formed was vaguely the shape of an egg cut the long way, but it would have covered the side of a six-story building. Two of them would enclose the crew module of Hermes, the skeleton of which was being assembled two miles away. The module would then be floated over to the main structure and attached as a unit. Other modules were taking shape similarly in various directions all around.

Linc and Danny, one of the second-part-basic rookies, in suits, were following the process from a "horse" hovering fifty feet off—a mobile maintenance platform consisting essentially of an open frame with an array of swivel jets and two crew stations, a carrier for tools and supplies, and a power unit. Danny updated the command file for the spider while Linc watched. It was his first excursion to any distance from the Shack, and he was still a shade apprehensive. Several yards away, their relief shift in the form of Arch and a rookie called Iram hung on a two-man scooter, waiting to move in.

"You don't need the F-normal bias so high," Linc said over the circuit. He was referring to the jet that maintained a slight force to hold the spider against the shell's surface. "Just a small bias will do it. The sensors will track any variation. It saves propellant and reduces drift."

"Okay, gotcha. . . . How's the gap?"

"About right for the curve. Watch your D reading. The nozzle's a little high."

Danny nodded behind his faceplate and made the adjustments. He was a farm boy from Washington State, always slow and methodical—but he usually got things right.

Arch's voice came through in Linc's helmet. "You guys about done yet?"

Linc ran his eyes one last time over the numbers showing on the screen pad strapped to his thigh and nodded. "It's running okay, but a little sluggish on the turns. I've logged it in. Okay, she's all yours." He used the pad to sign off the shift, verified that Arch had confirmed the changeover, and unsnapped his restraint harness on the horse. "Okay, Dan, let's get back to the Shack and hitch the next truck home to Grayling. I'm about ready for dinner."

Arch had pushed off of the scooter and was holding on with a hand, using his suit jet to steady it. Linc launched himself from the horse in a slow, turning motion that rotated him to slip neatly into the seat as he arrived. Arch took Linc's vacated position on the horse; then Danny and Iram switched places to complete the exchange. Linc detached the scooter from the safety line trailing from the structure they had been working on and used the steering gyros—quicker and simpler than juggling with jets, once you'd gotten the knack of them—to realign with the Construction Shack roughly a mile and a half away. "You on tight, Dan?"

"Secured and checked."

"Okay, see you guys back in the Tower later," Linc called as he opened up the thruster. One of the figures on the horse waved back as the scooter pulled away.

"Not me. I'll be heading straight for the pool," Arch's voice answered over the radio.

Linc and Danny moved away from the shell's reassuring bulk and out into the open star field. Suddenly the other constructions seemed far away and insignificant. Even Grayling Station was almost out of sight, partially obscured from this angle by the Construction Shack in between. Linc could remember how desperately exposed he had felt on his own first experience of this—like finding himself on the rock slab with just toeholds and a friction grip for his hands above a long drop for the first time.

Danny was evidently going through the same thing. "I remember when I went swimming out from the shore once as a kid and found I was in the middle of the river," his voice said in Linc's helmet. "It felt kinda like this."

"You'll get used to it," Linc told him.

"How long does it take?"

"How long did it take before you could swim across the river?"

"I did swim across—that first time. The trouble was that by then I was too scared to swim back."

"Well, out here it's easier. You won't drown if you get tired. The trouble is just in your mind." A year before, although he would never have admitted it, Linc had found guys like this intimidating, with their social backgrounds and education. Much of the tough exterior he'd maintained, and believed to be himself, had been overcompensation. Now he was teaching these guys.

"What made you decide to go out to the Zone?" Danny asked.

"At the time, I didn't know I was going there. It was one of those things, like, you know—you don't have much choice. One of those offers you can't refuse."

"Is it right you came through that place called Coulie in California, that some of the guys talk about?"

"Uh-huh."

"Is it like they say . . . that all of the people who went through there were in some kind of trouble?"

"I don't know. Nobody there ever talked about it." And Linc didn't especially feel like answering the questions he sensed were about to follow. "How about you?" he asked, heading Danny off instead.

"Oh . . . my folks broke up, and when I was asked which one I wanted to go with, I couldn't honestly answer either way. You know how it is—each of them used me as a sort of weapon against the other when they got in a fight, and I ended up terrified of both of them. Then one of the lawyers who was involved introduced me to someone who talked about opting out of it all and heading for the Outzone. . . ."

"It wouldn't have been a guy called Dr. Grober, by any chance, would it?" Linc asked. "White hair and a pink face. Always wears one of those dicky bow ties."

"No. It was some woman. Her name was Zeipel. Why?"

"It doesn't matter."

"Anyhow, it sounded better than anything else anyone was talking about. My parents both signed me off. . . . And here I am riding this thing with you up here, like the cow that jumped over the Moon."

The Construction Shack was now looming closer, its bulk throwing them suddenly into shadow from the Sun.

"So why the military?" Linc asked curiously.

"I was more interested in the computers—maybe getting into something like piloting one day too. They said a few years of this would be a good grounding in all of that. I think they want to put as many people as they can through this. The discipline probably helps later—you know, like how different it all must be out there."

"You should talk to Willie. He's got it all set up to be a pilot. He's got an uncle out in the Zone already who knows about all that. Willie's got the angles figured."

"Do you think—" Danny's voice cut off suddenly. A moment later, Linc felt and heard two urgent raps from behind on his helmet.

"What?"

Danny's voice came through, sharp with urgency. *"To your right—four o'clock, low!"*

Linc turned awkwardly to peer back past his shoulder. The main structure of Hermes lay in the direction that Danny had indicated. Part of it—a support pylon and a portion of girder work at its base—had torn away and was cartwheeling crazily, trailing lines convulsing in slow, whiplike motions. As Linc watched, one of them snagged around another nearby object, capturing it and pulling it into the tumbling pattern. Linc gave the scooter a power burst and gunned for the cover of the Shack. Seconds later, the site controller's voice barked in his helmet on the emergency band:

"Emergency! Emergency! We have a structure failure on the skeleton. A rotator is loose. Evacuate the area. Unshielded personnel be alert for debris."

Although the main mass of gyrating cables and metal seemed, if anything, to be shrinking, there was no telling which way detaching fragments might be thrown. Linc held a steady course for the homing beacon on the Shack's dark side, cutting in reverse at maximum only when he could see the inside of the bay, already opened and waiting. "This never happened in rivers!" Danny yelled as he thudded against Linc's back.

Linc took the scooter straight in, ignoring the outside parking rack. Suited figures helped them off and into one of the locks, shunting the scooter into a loading bay to keep the entrance clear for other vehicles converging outside. Once through the lock, Linc de-suited in the antechamber and hauled himself rapidly through corridors and connecting shafts to the communications area where the telecontrol consoles were located, which was where E Company was detailed to report.

Many of the other personnel seemed to be gathering there as well. Danny, not as accustomed yet to getting out of suits in a hurry or negotiating labyrinths of metal geometry in zero-g, arrived breathless and sporting a few bruises shortly after.

Linc sought out Captain Ullerman, who, for reasons not immediately clear, had been joined by two of the Construction Shack's senior officers from the Control Room. What were they doing here? A situation of this nature would be dealt with there, where all site operations were directed from. What was the relevance of a company-size outfit of cadets learning construction engineering? Willie and Flash were there; also some second-part rookies. They looked tense and pale—more so than the circumstances should have warranted.

Screens on the walls showed views from different directions of turning tangles of debris and lines. The initial configuration was coming apart. Another screen was open to the Control Room, showing the face of Director Earle, the Construction Shack's operations chief. Garbled reports were coming in over several audio channels at once. Several of the views, Linc realized as he tried to follow, seemed to be concentrating on one rotating form in particular: three masses connected by two lengths of linc, the whole oscillating and rebounding as it spun. It seemed to be receding.

Then the view snapped into clearer resolution as the recording camera zoomed closer in. The center mass was a mangled confusion of girders and metal latticework. One of the cables flailing from it was attached to a piece of machinery of some kind. The other was wrapped around a shape that Linc recognized as an effector capsule—an enclosed, mobile unit carrying up to four persons, used around the construction area to permit working in shirtsleeves via external manipulators.

At that moment an engineer at one of the consoles looked around at Ullerman and the two officers from the Control Room and indicated the picture that had stabilized on his screen. "We've got a connection now," he told them. The picture showed the head and shoulders of a girl wearing a cadet tunic. She seemed to be pinned against an instrument panel visible in the background. Her face had a vacant, bewildered expression. Blood was oozing from her nose and mouth, spreading all ways over her face in a ghastly pattern.

"What's happening?" Linc asked the others crisply.

"It's Nancy," one of the rookies gasped, horrified.

"Nancy! Nancy Powlin! Can you hear me in there?" Ullerman snapped into a mike.

Willie gestured first at a screen showing the lines and three masses tumbling, then at the internal view from the capsule that had just appeared. His eyes were wide with shock. "It got caught in the open," he told Linc hoarsely. "The shell's buckled and has to be compromised. Arvin's in there with two of the rookies. We're not getting any response. And it's heading away from us fast!"

CHAPTER TWENTY-NINE

THE pylon was a structural component designed to impart rigidity in a way somewhat like a tent pole. To achieve this, it was held in a flexed state by tension lines while its mountings and connections to the structure were secured. One of these lines had parted, and in recoiling had whiplashed through the partly completed supports, causing the pylon and some of the structure to break away. Arvin and the two rookies, Nancy and another called Cliff, had been snagged on their way out to haul materials from a floating supply dump left by the *Constellation*. Three emergency craft were in pursuit and one was closing in, but the pilot was baffled as to how to match course with such a wildly cavorting target. The masses and the two cables bounced like connected weights and springs as they spun, setting up complex wave motions that propagated back and forth, defying prediction.

"Nancy, now listen to me. I want you to take a long breath, and then concentrate on what you have to do. Okay? Don't look at any shiny surfaces. You're not hurt as bad as it seems. The force pattern is making it look worse. Do you understand, Nancy?" A doctor from the Construction Shack's Emergency Room had arrived in the communications area. Nancy had recovered her faculties partly, but she panicked when she saw a reflection of herself in a panel escutcheon. Now she was calming down again. Cliff had taken a knock on the head and seemed to be out cold. Arvin had been flung against the pilot's console, and according to Nancy was conscious but only semicoherent. She described his arm as being in an odd position and said he was in too much pain to move. Apparently the station director, Kelsoe, at Grayling, was now in touch with Director Earle, in the Shack's Control Room.

"She needs to enable the capsule's diagnostics for remote access so we can read them from here," the engineer who had gotten the view from inside said over his shoulder. "That capsule has to have taken some damage. We need a report on it."

"How does she do that?" the doctor asked.

"She has to activate the engineer's panel, then feed in some commands. Let me direct her."

The doctor looked back at the screen. "Nancy, do you hear me? . . . Nancy?" Nancy nodded once, blankly. "I want you to listen to Mr. Quine now. There are some things you have to do there for us. They're simple but *very* important. Now listen carefully. Okay?"

"Okay, Nancy, first, locate the *System Mode* switch, and make sure it's at 'CMD/MON.' Got that? Now go to your panel, and hit *Reset.* You should get the System Initialize screen. . . ."

Ullerman and the CR officers were watching another screen showing a transmission from the emergency flier trying to maneuver in. The capsule was visibly deformed and buckling where the turn of cable snaked around it. It grew larger, seemed to steady for a second or two, and then vanished suddenly in a different direction. On the engineer's screen, Nancy lurched to one side and clutched at a piece of bracing. A cry of pain, recognizably Arvin, sounded in the background. The view from the flier showed the piece of snarled wreckage enlarging suddenly as it hurtled toward the camera— "*Jesus!*"—then sliding away as the pilot evaded.

The pilot's voice came through again. "This is no good! It's like trying to second-guess two elastic yo-yos tied together."

Finally, the diagnostics of the capsule's systems came up on an auxiliary screen on Quine's console. "How's it looking?" Ullerman asked him.

The engineer scanned the numbers, then shook his head gravely. "Not good. Their main power's out. They're on emergency. . . . And the air reserve is way down. The shell is breached somewhere. Frankly, I'm surprised it's still in one piece. That cable wrapped around it might be all that's holding it together. But it can't take much more of this."

"Can she get them into suits?" one of the CR officers asked, turning from the screen that was showing Kelsoe and the others at Grayling. "It might give us more time to work something out."

The doctor shook his head. "No chance. She's still in shock. It's a miracle she's been able to do this much."

"Those fliers are gonna run out of range before much longer," the other CR officer said.

"Is there some way they can cut the lines?" somebody among Kelsoe's staff suggested from Grayling. They had been joined on the Bridge there by Colonel Weyer, chief of the military command at Grayling, who reported directly to Kelsoe.

"Maybe if we were equipped with laser artillery," the rescue pilot's voice answered, sounding sarcastic in his exasperation. "But we're not."

A numbed hush fell over the room. The juniors waited for the authorities to come up with something. The authorities were at a loss. All of them watched the screens, waiting for the tragedy to play itself out.

Then Linc looked across at Captain Ullerman. Ullerman sensed him from the corner of his eye and turned his head. "I think I know how we can cut the cable," Linc said. The CR officers pushed on the handrails to turn toward him. Linc hesitated. Ullerman nodded for him to go ahead. "Could we back up on that sequence we just had from the rescue flier?" Linc said, looking at the engineer, Quine. "I thought I saw something."

The officer in charge nodded. Quine played with keys on his console. The view coming in from the flier stopped for a second, then went into fast-motion reverse. Linc waited until the lattice section flew into view, almost filling the screen, then began shrinking. Running backward, it was the instant just before the pilot had been forced to evade. "Freeze it there," Linc said. "Now run it forward again slowly . . . more . . . a bit more. . . . Now hold." Linc pointed. Something bright yellow was lodged among the tangle of struts and girders. It was one of the remote-operated waldos used for general construction. "It's there at the other end of the line from the capsule," Linc said. "It has its own cutter. We can control it from here—right here in the Shack."

CHAPTER THIRTY

SEVERAL seconds of silence followed, echoed on the screen from Grayling, where Kelsoe and his staff had heard too. Everyone exchanged looks, waiting for someone else to voice the objection that had to be there but was too obvious to see just at that instant. Yet nobody did. Finally, the senior CR officer nodded curtly. "Do it," he said. Ullerman looked around uncertainly as the realization hit him that the onus was suddenly on him to take it from here.

"Let Linc try," Willie prompted, with uncharacteristic forwardness from among those to the side. "He's the best telecontrol man we've got."

Ullerman pulled himself together. "Get an identification from the assignment list of which waldo that is," he said to

Quine and indicated one of the telecontrol consoles. "Then get a link from it to Unit 9 there."

Not waiting to be told, Linc hauled himself over to the TC console that Ullerman had specified, clipped into the operator harness, and began pulling on the gloves. One of the others, spurred into action by his move, plugged in the helmet for him and lowered it over his head. "Do we know if that waldo out there is still working?" Linc heard somebody asking as darkness blotted out the scene in the room.

"We'll soon find out," Quine's voice replied.

The start-up page appeared in Linc's visual field. He stepped rapidly through the familiar activation routine—"It's checking positive," Quine's voice said from somewhere, sounding crisper now that there was something to do—and suddenly Linc was out in space.

But hurled into an experience unlike any he had known before. For a moment he thought he was going to be sick. The stars around him careened in a wild, irregular motion which, although it was purely visual, caused his stomach to churn and threw his balance reflexes into chaos. It was like being on a runaway roller coaster bucking and falling in three dimensions. Although the waldo was still anchored, Linc found himself clutching instinctively to hold on with the manipulators, via the gloves.

Ullerman's voice came through the helmet. "We have a slave off your visual, Linc. It looks good. You copy?"

"I'm reading you."

"How does it feel?"

"Rough."

"You need to get to the other end of the line. The engineers don't want to risk the recoil of cutting it where you are. Can you do that, Linc?"

That was all he needed, Linc thought, fighting the heaves still assailing his stomach. "I'll try, sir."

"There probably isn't a lot of time. . . ."

"Sys on," Linc ordered. "Manipulator both, power gain to max." A virtual gauge superposed upon his vision confirmed the setting. He gripped the structure immediately in front of him. "Anchor, disengage. Sys off." Now he was attached only by the metal-fingered hands, clamping at full power. The forces feeding back through the gloves made him feel as if he were hanging onto a treetop swishing in a gale. The waldo swung away from the girder like a flag from a mast, then crashed back against it as the structure changed direction. Linc marveled that its joints were able to take the stress.

Cautiously releasing one hand, he extended it to a new position. Miraculously, the single remaining hand held. Making certain the first was firmly secured before releasing the other, he pulled in and turned the waldo slowly until he was looking out along the cable that connected to the capsule. The line in between snaked up and down and from side to side in curves flowing first toward him and then back again, while the stars continued their deranged dance in the background. That was the gap he was going to have to cross. For a moment he caught a glimpse of the rescue flier whirling past in the distance; then it was gone again. From nowhere the preposterous thought formed in his mind that if he ever did go climbing with Patch in the mountains again, at least it wouldn't be like this. Alternating his grasps with slow deliberation, he began hauling himself hand-over-hand out onto the line writhing across empty space.

"I just want you to know we're with you every inch of the way, son," a high-ranking voice in his helmet informed him.

Yeah, right. . . . Linc was having to concentrate too much to reply.

The ride on the piece of debris had been nothing compared with the line. Linc was hurled back and forth, feeling like a fly on a whip that was being cracked. And yet, as his confidence in the waldo increased, and he began getting the hang of coordinating his moves, he managed to move faster. He was past the halfway point when Ullerman's voice came through once more.

"Linc, do you read?"

"I read."

"You're doing just great. Nancy has got a hand camera operating in there. The doc says that Arvin's shoulder looks as if it's out. Arvin's head has cleared a bit, and he wants to talk to you. Can we patch him through?"

"Right now? I am kinda busy."

"He's being insistent."

"Make it quick, then."

One side of Linc's visual field became an internal shot from the capsule, showing Arvin clinging with his good arm to the pilot's support frame. The other side of him was crookedly misshapen. His face was strained and whiter than Linc had ever seen it. A cut in his arm was oozing globs of blood that drifted lazily in the air like slow-motion details from a violent action movie. "Am I through?" he asked in a wheezy voice.

"You're patched into the waldo channel," someone answered.

"I can see you, Arv," Linc confirmed. "I'm right outside, almost there now."

"I guess I flunked pilot's school, eh?" Arvin said.

"I wouldn't say you had a lot to do with it. We'll get you out of there, don't worry."

"Look, Linc . . . just in case this doesn't work out . . ." Arvin winced and had to pause to regather his voice. He gasped several breaths. "There's something that you have to know. . . . It's important."

"We don't really have time for this," Quine's voice cut in.

Linc decided Arvin was partly delirious. "Arv, save it. You can tell me about it back in Grayling. I got work to do, buddy. Sys on. Com out," he instructed. The scene from inside the capsule vanished.

Now there were just ten yards or so to go. The capsule's mass was less than that of the wreckage at the end Linc had started out from, and its oscillations correspondingly more violent. Its outside was buckled where the cable had crushed it. Fortunately, the capsule was designed with a double hull. Getting the knack now, Linc was able to use the surges in the cable to help him along. He was almost there when a new voice came through.

"Cadet Marani?"

"Yes?"

"This is the chief engineering officer from the Bridge at Grayling."

"Sir?"

"You're just approaching the capsule, is that right? We've been following you on the shots coming back from the rescue fliers."

"Almost there now, sir."

"We have a Doppler-radar fix on you from here. Look, I don't know if you follow this, but the center of mass there is moving away from us at a considerable velocity. However, due to the rotation, the end of the cable that you're at periodically traces a reverse trajectory that almost cancels it. That means that if you cut the line at the right moment—which we'll tell you from here—the capsule should come out of it practically dead in the water, on little more than a slow drift relative to us. Do you understand?"

"Anchor on the capsule side. . . . Don't make the cut until you say so."

"You've got it."

The way a wheel rolls, the axle carries the whole assembly forward, while the point on the rim immediately below is actually rotating backward at the same speed. The two velocities cancel, and so the rim of the wheel doesn't slip. The CEO was saying they were going to try to lose the capsule's velocity by detaching it a an instant when a comparable state of affairs existed.

Linc finished the final yards swinging almost evenly, like an orangutan coasting the trees. He hauled himself around the mess of cable and anchored the waldo on one of the capsule's thruster mounts. Relief swept through him as he felt himself become a part of something solid again. "Sys on. Control, right appendage. Disenable manipulator. Enable cutter. Sys off." His right arm had become a cutter. He positioned it around the base of the cable. "In position and ready," he reported into his helmet mike.

Voices came across the gap from Grayling.

"Delta—vee two-twenty, reducing."

"Here's that harmonic again. This could be it. . . ."

"One-eighty, one-fifty. . . . The derivative's not leveling. It looks like we're going all the way down."

"Standing by, Marani?"

"I read. Standing by."

"Under a hundred. Good enough?"

"We can go more. It's not bottoming yet."

"Forty . . . thirty . . . twenty-five . . . twenty . . . fifteen. . . . Look at that. It's flat. You won't do any better. It's gonna pick up again now."

"Okay, cut it!"

Linc snipped two of his fingers together; fifty miles way across space, metal shears cut through braided steel almost an inch thick. . . .

And almost instantly, his world returned to sanity.

Like a flurry of snow being called to order, the stars suddenly stabilized, and the cable became part of a spinning anomaly shrinking and vanishing rapidly into the distance. Linc found himself on the outside of the capsule, drifting gently against a backdrop of space that was normal again. Then it all vanished abruptly, and he was back, dripping with sweat, inside the Construction Shack.

The three rescue craft moved in and enveloped the stricken capsule in a plastic bag, which was quickly sealed and filled with air. Medics and rescue techs were already in the lock, waiting to enter. They found the three occupants unconscious. The slackening of the cable had allowed a tear in the inner hull to open, losing the last reserves of air. In the engineer's estimation, the remaining supply had by that time run down to less than five minutes' worth in any case. They were rushed back to Grayling, Arvin with a dislocated shoulder and strained back, Cliff with a concussion, Nancy still in acute shock, and all of them with multiple cuts and bruises. But none of the damage was serious or permanent, and all three were expected to come out of it just fine.

Linc earned himself a new nickname: *Bronco.*

CHAPTER THIRTY-ONE

LINC'S sixteenth birthday came while he was out in space at Grayling. Julie gave him a tie clip in the design of an anvil. "Because I know you'll create art in metal some day," she told him. It was the perfect gift. Linc had no idea where she had gotten it. This was the first time he'd had a birthday gift from anyone outside his immediate family—and that had been only when he was a kid.

They had met for lunch in the cafeteria in North Tower, where Julie worked. She was helping with the tending of patients now. Linc had completed his construction basics and was on a day of free time before starting a class on remote-directed space-assault robots. The joke among the other cadets was that he should have been teaching it.

"How's Arvin doing?" Linc asked across the table as he dug his fork into a plate of mixed salad. Cliff and Nancy had been kept under observation in the sick bay until the previous day, and then released. Linc had received an E-mail from Nancy's parents in Maine, thanking him for what he had done. They also sent one to Arvin to let him know they didn't hold him accountable for the accident. Nancy had no doubt sent them a line giving all the news. Although the authorities that ran Grayling didn't go out of their way to publicize their activities, personnel there were not expected to cut themselves off from the world. Censorship wouldn't have been consistent with what the Outzone was all about.

"He's doing okay," Julie replied. "The doctor saw him this morning. It wouldn't surprise me if he's up and about this afternoon. It'll be a while before he can use that arm properly again, though."

"It's good he's so much better." Linc speared a green olive and ate it.

Julie eyed him over her sandwich. "Does this mean the standoff that's been going on between you two might finally be over? It'd be about time."

"Hey, I seem to go through this with everybody. Talk to him about it, not me. I've been approachable all the time." Linc shook his head. "He's still got some kind of problem. I've given up trying to figure it."

"So might you if you had to walk around Seville Trace with your face looking like a peach that got run over," Julie said, chiding mildly.

"Don't try to hang that one on me. It was squaring up an account that needed squaring. He knew that."

"Was it really that important?"

"It's the way I do business." Linc started to look irritable.

Julie smiled resignedly and reached across to squeeze his hand. "Let's not spoil lunch by going off into all that now, especially on your birthday," she said. "The *Armstrong* will be arriving in less than two weeks. Then we'll be on our way at last. Let's think about that."

Linc stared at her, then let go of the tenseness that had started building for a moment and grinned. He chewed a mouthful of salad and squeezed her hand back. It felt soft and smooth, tempting all the impulses of the age he was at. But he had held off from pushing things in that direction. They hadn't talked much about it. There seemed to be an unspoken understanding that it was something they both wanted to save until their new life in the Outzone began. Maybe it was silly to even think about at such an age, but the possibility had crossed Linc's mind of starting a family when they got there. Or was it silly only by the standards of the dying culture they were leaving? Nature and biology's opinion on the matter was clear. By all accounts, the need for people in the Outzone was insatiable, and marriages and pairings were encouraged at ages that would be considered preposterous, unnatural even, on Earth. Perhaps that was what drew people there unconsciously, instinctively—especially young people. The spirit that drove the Outzone was that of life and birth and growth. What lay behind was slowly succumbing to stagnation, decay, and death.

Three cadets at the far end of the room got up to leave. "Watch it guys, it's the hero," one of them said as they came to the table where Linc and Julie were sitting. The other two walked by muttering:

"Hero, hero. . . ."

"Hero, hero. . . ."

One of them gave Linc a light, approving clap on the shoulder as he passed. This would go on for a few days yet, Linc could see. He shook his head and looked at Julie helplessly. She smiled and let go of his hand to resume eating her sandwich.

"It's going to be so different out there," she said. "Think of it—where people value the things that are actually worth something. On Earth they've forgotten how to make everything except money. But what good is it if there's nothing worthwhile left to buy?"

Linc stared at her. Wasn't that about what Dr. Grober had said in different words? It seemed an eternity ago now. And the mysterious "Mr. Black" at Coulie? . . . Angelo had said it in deeds, not words. It was the first time Linc had gotten the feeling he was beginning to understand what they had meant.

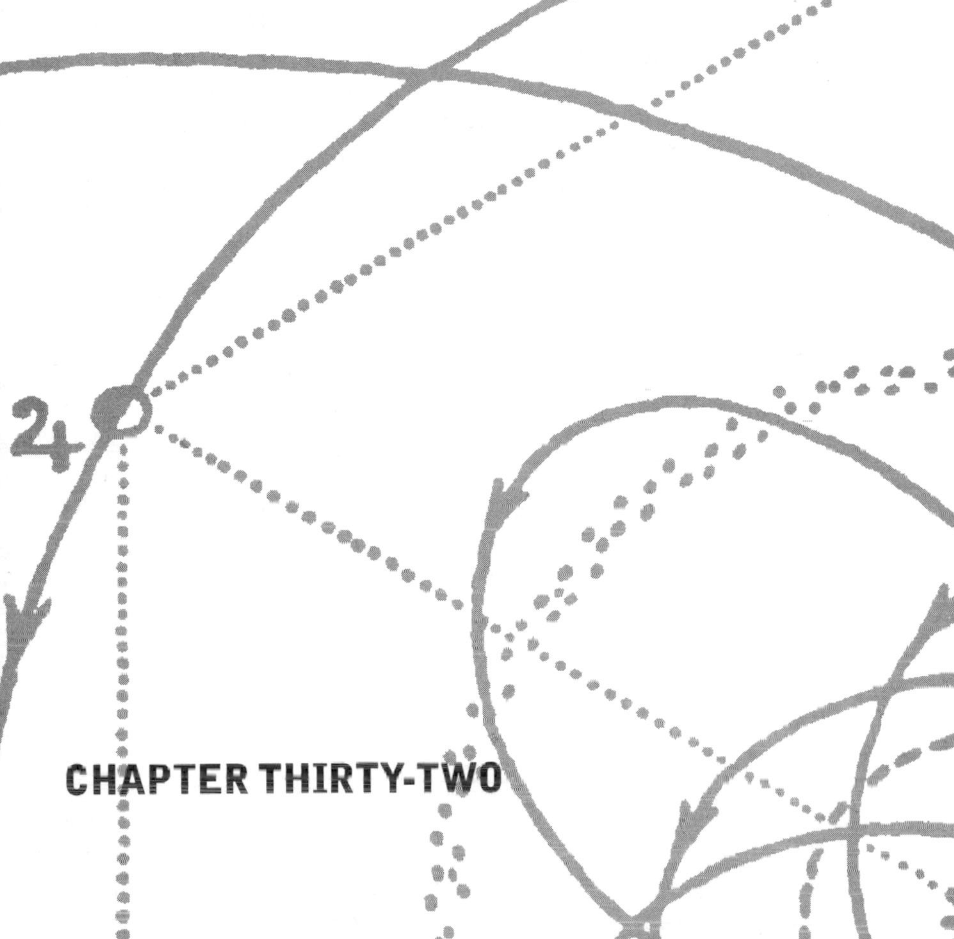

CHAPTER THIRTY-TWO

LATER that afternoon, after Linc had returned to the South Tower and was debating with Flash and Arch whether to take in a movie or visit the Low-g Court, Linc's pager—a concession allowed senior cadets—buzzed, and an adjutant informed him that he was to report to Colonel Weyer's conference room at once. Weyer was another remote figure as far as the cadets were concerned. They saw him at inspections or when he gave occasional pep talks, but it was rare for them to have dealings with him directly. He had already complimented Linc personally on his initiative in the capsule incident. Linc could only surmise that the summons had to do with some kind of follow-up to that.

"They're gonna give you a medal," Arch said; then he frowned. "Do they give medals to cadets?"

"I dunno," Flash answered. "Come to that, has the Zone ever awarded anything to anybody? It's never been involved in real combat."

"Dierot was in more than a few battles," Arch said.

"They were French or something."

"For valor in the face of the enemy," Arch recited. "That's what it'll say on it, Linc."

"There wasn't any valor involved," Linc pointed out as he finished knotting his tie and checked his hair in a mirror. "I was safe inside the Shack all the time."

"Maybe they're going to name one of the new ships after you then," Flash said. "The *Linc Marani*. . . . I kinda like that. Do you have a middle initial, Linc—you know, like they do with the *Armstrong?* It sounds neater."

Linc snorted as he buttoned and straightened his tunic. "More likely they'll name the waldo after me," he threw back, putting on his cap as he left the room.

Colonel Weyer had a solemn, thick-lipped face with dark, protruding eyes, and slicked-back dark hair showing gray streaks at the temples. He was sitting at the head of the table dominating the conference room when Linc was shown in by a secretary. Two staff officers, one on either side, were sitting across the corners from him. Captain Ullerman was next along the table beside one of them. Opposite him, to Linc's surprise, was Arvin, his arm in a black sling. Next to Ullerman was a man wearing a crew officer's uniform, the shoulder insignia identifying him as from the Engineering Division. Arvin looked strained. Files lay open on the table in front of Weyer and Ullerman. One of the staff officers had an open screen pad, the other, an old-style notebook and pen. The two staff officers and the crew engineering officer, whom Linc had seen around but never had reason to be involved with more closely, looked at him curiously. "This is the young man who not only cut the cable but was the person who spotted the waldo and thought of using it, " Weyer said by way of introduction.

"Congratulations," one of the staff officers murmured.

"A quick piece of thinking," the engineering officer said.

"Thank you," Linc responded.

"Do you think you could use people like him?" Weyer asked the engineering officer.

"No question. With the ship construction that's being planned, we could use a hundred." There seemed to be some significance to the question that Linc was unable to grasp yet. He was ordered to ease and invited to sit down, which he did, at the far end of the table. Weyer drew the open folder in front of him a few inches nearer and stared down at it, as if to focus attention on the business at hand.

"Senior Cadet Marani," he said, looking up. "You came to us through what we call the 'special preparatory course,' Phase One at Camp Coulie, California, where you were made a section leader and received excellent appraisals, and Phase Two at Seville Trace in Texas."

"Yes, sir."

"We have the reports here from your principal Phase Two coach, Mr. Summer, and the other specialist instructors you were with there. It seems that you had thoughts about training in precision engineering crafts—maybe for instrument work or tool prototyping."

"That's correct, sir."

"Could I throw in a word here?" the engineering officer asked Weyer.

The colonel waved a hand. "Sure."

The officer looked back at Linc. "I'm curious as to why that was," he said. "Can you tell us?"

It was an unusual and unexpected question. Linc frowned, trying hard not to appear dumb, and answered as best he could with no time for thought or preparation.

"I guess . . . it was the first time in my life that I'd ever *created* anything that was any good to people—you know, with my own hands. I'd never really seen inside machinery before—engines, gear systems . . . like, really seen inside. And it just fascinated me. The thought of being able to make parts that exact, out of just . . . lumps of metal. . . . And then they all fit together and actually work. It was like learning an art or something." He wondered if he was perhaps starting to come across a bit too lyrically and spread his hands to cut it off there. "Anyhow, that was what I wanted to do." The engineering officer nodded, smiling faintly.

Weyer resumed, "And what happened to change that hope?"

"I, er . . . I guess I just couldn't handle the math and the geometric side of it," Linc answered.

"Could you elaborate a little, please?"

Linc was at a loss to imagine what could have brought all this up now. But there was no choice but to go along with it. "At the end of Phase Two we had a practical test," he said. "A set of parts that had to be machined and finished. Not exactly what you'd call the most complicated, I guess, but there were some dimensions that the drawings didn't give—that you had to work out. Thinking back about it, a big part of the idea might have been to see if your mind worked the right way." He shrugged and sighed. "I guess mine didn't."

"The results that you turned it were not up to an acceptable standard, was that so?" Weyer said, checking his file again.

"That's correct, sir."

Weyer sat forward to rest his elbows on the table. "And were you surprised?"

This was even stranger than the previous questions. Linc hesitated.

"Be honest, Marani," one of the staff officers put in. "This isn't a modesty contest."

Okay, they had asked him. "Well, yes, I was," Linc replied. "As a matter of fact, I thought I'd done pretty good. The instructor had been telling me I was a natural."

"A pretty devastating letdown," the other staff officer, who hadn't spoken so far, commented.

"I've pulled through worse, sir," was all Linc could think of to reply.

Weyer stared at him, nodding slowly to himself in a way that seemed to say he was satisfied. Then he turned, for the first time, to Arvin, who had been looking progressively more miserable as the exchange continued. "And now, Senior Cadet Lomax. Would you kindly repeat for Mr. Marani what you disclosed to us earlier."

Arvin stared down woodenly and began in a little more than a mumble, "The test pieces that were turned in—"

Weyer interrupted. "Don't tell the table. Tell *him.*"

Arvin licked his lips and raised his head. He took a long breath and looked Linc in the face. "The test pieces that were turned in under your name were not the ones that you had made. Welsh switched them for some junk practice pieces that were in the store. It was me. I got him to do it."

Linc could only stare for what must have been ten seconds or more. "*What?*" was all he could manage, even then. It still hadn't registered fully. The others in the room waited, giving him time. He shook his head as if to help it clear. "Then . . . what happened to mine?"

"I told Welsh to get rid of them. . . ." Arvin half lifted a hand from the table in a plea for some kind of understanding, even a little. "It was right after that thing, you know, in the gym. I was . . ." He let it go, realizing he was just sounding lame.

Colonel Weyer allowed a short silence. Then he asked, "Do you have anything you'd like to say at this point, Marani?"

The "at this point" sounded like a hint. Linc took it and replied, "I think I need a little time to think about that, sir."

Weyer seemed to have been hoping for that and nodded. "Do you want to talk the matter over privately with anyone here?"

"I'd rather be alone . . . thank you . . . sir."

"Very well." Weyer rose from his chair. "I have a few pressing things to do. Lomax will wait in one of the detention rooms, unlocked. Captain Ullerman will post a guard to prevent intrusions. We'll reconvene, gentlemen, in one hour."

CHAPTER THIRTY-THREE

LINC wandered around the corridors, only half aware of his surroundings and the greetings tossed at him by others he passed. Perhaps drawn by some unconscious instinct, he found himself finally in the observation room in the outer hull, from where he had gazed out across space that evening that seemed long ago now, when he arrived at Grayling.

At first he felt nothing but anger and the impulse to hit back. By the code of the streets he had grown up in, there was nothing to think about. He had been wronged, and now he had the power to get even. To do otherwise would be not only weak but dishonorable. That was the way he did business. So why had he asked Weyer for time to think?

As the reflexive emotions subsided and relinquished control, he began to realize that other parts of him existed now that made it a more complex issue. He was no longer a creature of those streets. He was learning there were other ways of life, in which people practiced a different kind of business. That was what they had been forcing him to see at Coulie. He thought of Angelo and the things he had risked or given up in order to help those like Linc see. Why should Angelo have done that? By the old code, he owed none of them anything, stood to get nothing out of it. The answer could only be that there was much that was worthwhile to be gained by *his* code. Could Linc learn to understand that also?

And then Linc did something he had never been able to, or would even have comprehended, before in his life. He turned the situation around in his mind and tried not just to see it but to *feel* it from the other side.

It had been a low, cheap trick on Arvin's part, sure. But that had been another world ago, as Dr. Grober had said. This was now. Yes, Arvin had been mad enough and hurt enough and mean enough to want to deprive Linc of the thing that Linc had wanted most. But then Linc thought of the humiliation Arvin had chosen to eat in the campfire incident rather than risk being RPO'd, how he'd surprised everyone by the way he pulled his team together at Coulie. The chance for this new life was something that *he* desperately wanted too, every bit as much as Linc. And yet he had come to Weyer now, prepared to put all that on the line in order to set right what needed to be set right. Linc realized then what it must have taken for him to do that. The thug who had pushed Kew off the seat of the bus on the way up from Fresno would never have been capable of it. The enraged animal that had slunk away from the confrontation at the campfire couldn't have conceived of it. So Arvin had been learning and changing, too.

Then he thought back to Julie and the way they'd talked about how different their life would be out there. What kind of life would it be, he wondered, if, at his first test, he took with him in his mind everything they'd thought they were getting away from? What would it mean if he let revenge be his first meaningful choice before they had even begun. He tried to make himself think the way he imagined somebody who knew how to live out there in the Outzone would have to think. . . .

And suddenly there was nothing more to think about.

He got up, left the observation room, and headed back toward the Admin Section and Colonel Weyer's office.

"It was a different world then. We were all different people," Linc told the room. "I can't really see that there'd be a lot of point in dragging something back up now and making a big thing out of it, when it doesn't belong here. I think it took a lot of guts for him to come and say what he said, and that's the way we should be looking at it. If my case gets to be reconsidered . . . then that's good enough. I know that what he did was serious. But then, it's Arvin who's trying to put things right too. I'd prefer it be left at that. . . . Sir."

"I take it, then, that your own recommendation would be for leniency in view of changed circumstances," Weyer said.

Linc closed his eyes, hoped it was for the best, and nodded. "That's right, sir."

"Thank you, Cadet Marani. You are dismissed."

And that was when Linc learned something else. The look he got from Arvin as he left the room was worth more than any satisfaction he could have felt from seeing him destroyed.

The verdict was announced the next day. Since the incident had occurred before Arvin's admission to the service, he had not been under the jurisdiction of the Outzone's armed forces, and there was therefore no case to answer. The matter was closed. Linc had seen enough before to have no doubt that had they wished to do so, the lawyers could have found equally good reasons for ruling completely the other way.

As for Linc, he was told his situation was to be reviewed, and he would be advised of the outcome shortly. In the meantime his place on the *Neil A. Armstrong* was confirmed, as were the places of the other cadets who had made senior. So was

Julie's. Both of them would be going to Coombe, on the Jovian moon Callisto, the main transit base that most of the new arrivals to the Outzone passed through. Prior to the launch date, he was entitled to a five-day special leave to Earth to say farewells and so on. Since Julie had no family of her own she particularly wanted to visit, she readily agreed to accompany him. And his relationship with Arvin had changed so much that Linc invited him to go along too.

It wasn't just a celebration of their new buddiness and friendship. Linc figured that if he was going back to the neighborhood he'd come from, it might be wise to take along all the backup he could get.

CHAPTER THIRTY-FOUR

LINC didn't know if it was his imagination, but the streets seemed to have gotten older and dirtier—more so, surely, then was possible in the time that had gone by. What he remembered as the center of where the action was, and where all of life happened, had turned into tired and shabby remnants of an age that was running down. Had the storefronts always been so grubby, with their cloudy windows, halfhearted displays, the paint around the doors dulled and peeling like the once-high hopes of some forgotten opening day long ago? Had trash always stunk like this, piled in alleys and strewn along the gutters?

Above it all, high-rental buildings that had once thrust proudly toward the sky crumbled silently amid the winds, the rain, and the corrosive fumes eating into them. They had degenerated into cheap hotels and apartments while business fled the cities for manicured office parks by the interstates. But the people no longer stopped to gaze at these buildings, in any case. The figures on the sidewalks hurried on, avoiding each other's eyes, enwrapped in their own isolation. Even those who stood or walked together aimed words at each other from behind facades that had become so second nature that even they themselves now mistook them for the persons atrophying within. A city of brooding shells, inhabited by beings who hid inside shells.

"Hey, don't tell me that's . . . It is! Hey, Linc! How's it been going?" One of the two hookers standing outside Ozzie's Bar stepped forward as he approached—except that it was no longer Ozzie's but had been given a face-lift and become the Paradise Lounge. Linc recognized her as Irene, who used to be a cocktail waitress at The Domino along the next block, and before that, in some other city, a clerk in a shoe shop whose owner had packed the shelves with empty boxes so customers wouldn't know how run-down the stock was.

"Say, Irene, get a look at you!"

"We heard how you got pulled after that sting they set up. I guess you're back out now, then, huh? Did they slice you some time off or something?"

Linc smiled faintly. The girls liked to stay friendly with neighborhood muscle who carried pocket phones. You never knew when a trick might turn nasty or decide he was due extra time. "Yeah, I suppose you could say that," he said.

Irene put a hand on his shoulder and looked him up and down. "It can't have been too bad. You're looking in good shape, you know that? . . . Although, I can't say the clothes are really 'you,' know what I mean? Is that something they gave you? The haircut too. You musta just got out."

Linc had on a low-key, regular-cut navy jacket, blue-gray pants, and a dark-blue shirt with tie. It was just a casual combination that felt comfortable to travel in. Although there was no bar on wearing uniform, he had preferred not to flaunt one. It would have felt like advertising a big difference that existed between himself and everyone else now—as if he had somehow risen above them all. At least, he hadn't wanted to risk their seeing it that way.

"I'm just kinda visiting before moving on," Linc said. "I have to go back. Then they'll be sending me a lot farther." He waited for a hint of curiosity, a question, maybe? . . . But Irene's eyes left him to scan a man walking past in a business suit, automatically assessing for signs of a potential client. Linc decided to let it drop. "So how's it been with you?" he asked. "Moving on to a different neck of the woods too, eh?"

Irene shrugged, pouting a mouth that had too much lipstick. "The money and the hours are better, and it's easier on the feet," she said. "What can I tell you? It's just like any other job after a while. You wake up, you make money, you owe it to somebody for this or for that, you eat, you go to sleep again, and one day you die. What else is there?"

What else is there? The words repeated themselves in Linc's mind. *What can I tell you?* Irene had said. What was there for him even to have begun telling her.

He looked at her more closely. It probably wouldn't have been so obvious to him before, but he could still see behind the purple lips, the paint, and the overdone mascara, the shoe-shop girl who had run away from home to do better. Like Ozzie's bar with its gaudy new front and colored lights, she was fooling the world that didn't know her with what the outside pretended to be.

Irene indicated her companion, who was staring across the street vacantly, chewing a wad of gum. "This is Orla. She's new around here—sharing with me till she gets her own place."

Linc nodded. "Hi." Orla smiled back. She was young, and from the look of her, probably tripped out on something. Not a word, not a thought. Neither necessary nor relevant, so why bother? Available merchandise on the block.

"Linc's one of the guys from around. He's been away for a while, you know—like out of circuit. He's okay."

Orla blew a bubble of gum and popped it. "I'm getting hungry," she said.

Linc glanced away along the street. "Well, I've got things to do and not a lot of time. It was good running into you."

"You going back soon?" Irene asked.

"'Fraid so—out of here tonight." Linc and the others had allowed time for a little last-chance-on-Earth-for-a-while relaxation before shipping back. Marlene, still in an up-again, down-again, on-again, off-again relationship with Arvin, had been added to the party at the last moment to make up a foursome, and Rocky and Liz would be joining them after a quick trip to Liz's hometown in Connecticut.

Irene looked disappointed. "Oh, that soon, huh? Well . . . let's hope they don't keep you out there too long. So, take it easy, eh?"

"And you. . . . Good meeting you, Orla."

Orla blew him another bubble with her gum.

CHAPTER THIRTY-FIVE

ON the way down from Grayling, Linc had fantasized about reappearing as the adventurer returned from afar, astounding his friends with accounts of places he had been and things he had seen that were beyond their wildest imagination. He would tell them about the things that were happening beyond the Moon, and open their eyes to the realms of wonder and opportunity waiting out there. Bringing enlightenment like some kind of crusader, his last task before departing would be to spread the word and the vision so that others might follow.

By the time he arrived at what had been one of his regular hangouts—the back room behind Big Dino's diner, where you could kill an hour over a coffee or even a real beer as long as you were willing to say you'd brought it yourself—the thought was already as dead as the chicken cuts stacked in Dino's freezer. The torch Linc had carried fizzled out under a rolling tsunami of realizations of things that would never change—a process otherwise known as a confrontation with reality.

Chips Reid was in the center of one of the wooden benches flanking the room's two tables when Linc appeared from the passageway past the kitchen. He still dressed to try and look like a big shot and was holding a bottle of Bud. Chips was few years older than Linc and had gotten the name after a scam he'd been mixed up in that involved selling suckers fake gambling chips, supposedly stolen. Next to him was Joe Belluni—nicknamed, inevitably, Baloney—already arrested four times (that had been the score when Linc was last around) for break-ins and larceny but never convicted. Larry, "The Boot," was sitting on the bench opposite. Larry's specialty was demonstrating that having strong door locks didn't do a lot of good if the doorframe wasn't at least as strongly fixed into the wall. Two others were with them that Linc didn't recognize: a sharp-faced youth, maybe twentyish, who could have been Puerto Rican, and a blond-haired guy not unlike Arvin in appearance but fatter.

Linc had to speak before recognition dawned on them. "Hi, Chips. Joe. . . . Larry. . . ." It was the hair and the clothes. Evidently the street girls had a better eye for picking out faces.

There was a moment of silence. they, "My God! It's Linc Marani back from the joint!" Chips waved an arm magnanimously, as if he were ushering a big spender into a plush club that he owned, not the back room of somebody else's backstreet meatball restaurant. Linc pulled a chair over from the other table and sat down.

Joe Baloney made an appealing gesture at the others. "He just breezes in off the street . . . like it was only yesterday that he walked out. So, it's great to see you again, Linc." Linc had always had time for Joe. He always got the feeling that Joe would listen and try to understand when Linc attempted to explain something, whereas most others just returned blank stares.

Larry just nodded. He never said much. Linc had the impression he wouldn't have shown surprise if the president of the country had suddenly walked in. Fat Blondie nodded too, but without changing expression. The Puerto Rican just glowered suspiciously.

Chips went on, "So when did they let you out, Linc? We heard it, like, you know, around, that you'd gone down a big hole in the ground because you wouldn't deliver any names the way that thing they pulled was supposed to collect. Clay and Slam are still on ice, and, hey, they didn't even have the contacts. . . ." He seemed to remember the two new faces suddenly, and waved. "Oh, and these are Lou and Gomez, who drifted in from D.C. a while back. Linc's a squeeze man who's been around here forever, guys. He got busted, when? . . . It must have been around a year ago, in a setup operation they pulled. . . . So what happened, man? Did you ever see any more of those other two that you worked that job with?"

Linc shook his head. "I guess we must have gone different ways. There was a special kind of program they've got, that some people got a chance to try for. Well, it was clear what the alternative was, so I went for it."

"Yeah, well, I always thought that Clay and Slam were losers anyway," Chips said, waving a hand dismissively. "You remember that time Clay was going to torch Velo's car over that loan thing? I mean *he* wants to send Velo a message? Come on, gimme a break. The only thing that amazes me is that Clay's still alive."

Linc wasn't interested in hearing replays of anecdotes that had already been old long ago. "So what's new?" he asked.

Chips stared down as his hands, spreading his fingers. He was wearing a lot of rings these days, Linc noticed. "Kyle's still around, running the collections. . . ." Chips paused, as if considering whether to confide something weighty. "As a matter of fact, we might be working something out—you know, sharing some of the action. He made me this proposition. . . ."

It was strange. Linc had practically forgotten about Kyle. He could remember nights when he had lain awake nursing the rage that had burned in him, consoling himself by rehearsing in his mind how he would get even. And not just with Kyle but also the man called Carolton, whom Breece had said Kyle worked for. But somehow over the months that had slowly changed . . . and now it just didn't matter anymore. Linc had seen things that Kyle could never know. He could no longer hate a man he didn't envy.

Chips mistook his silence for resentment. "Well, it did leave a kind of a hole that needed filling when you evaporated," he said. "Business has to go on, and all that. . . . We could talk about cutting you back in, I guess. Want me to mention it to him?"

"He's scum," Linc said. "The worst. Take some good advice: Have nothing to do with him."

Chips looked offended. "Hey, Linc, are you forgetting who you're talking about? That could get somebody into bad health around here. I mean, I know you got a bad rap, but he did what he could—"

"He didn't do anything. I was thrown overboard."

"What are you talking about, Linc? The pukes had it in for you from the start. Kyle told me the story. They wouldn't even give you bail. He had a lawyer on it practically full-time."

"He lied. The package he's selling kids is a line. He's using them as expendables to save his soldiers. If you want to do the kids a favor, spread it around. If you want to do yourself one, walk."

Chips stared at Linc as if he had taken leave of his senses. "Phew! . . . I mean, man, you really don't care about laying it on." He meant Linc's talking this way in front of people he didn't know. "You must be forgetting some of the basics about staying smart around here, know what I mean?"

"It doesn't matter to me," Linc said. "Three days from now I'll be going back."

"You mean to that special program you mentioned?" Joe said.

Linc nodded. "Uh-huh."

Joe seemed curious. Or maybe he just wanted to head Linc and Chips away from a course that could get acrimonious.

"What is it, exactly? One of these rehab things they have, where shrinks ask you questions all the time, and you get to be a gardener or something?"

Linc shook his head. "No, it doesn't have anything to do with the state, the feds, or anything like that. It's not really a rehab trip. More a way of starting out again all over."

"Staring what out again?" Joe asked. Chips looked huffy. He didn't seem to like Linc's walking in and getting all the attention.

"Your life," Linc said. "If nobody's got a place for you here but they figure you can be something that you haven't discovered yet, they'll move you out to where things are different. And that way, maybe you find out."

Chips made a face. "Who? Move you out where? What are we talking about here?"

"The Outzoners—you know, out there in space. It's like the government hands you over."

"You're going out *there*?" Chips looked perplexed. Given a week, he would have had trouble forming something more meaningful to say on such a topic.

"From Yucatán three days from now," Linc said. "Then shipping out from lunar orbit another three days after that. That's why I came back—for a last look around. . . . You know the kind of thing."

"Isn't it all supposed to be a bit crazy out there?" Joe said guardedly. "There was something about it on TV—like they don't want to trade, won't let anyone put any big money into what they're doing. It sounded like some kind of religious-cult thing."

Linc looked at him strangely. He had never thought of it that way. "I guess in a way you could say it is," he said.

Chips threw up both hands to recapture his audience. "Hell, if they won't let people put money in, that has to say it all. You can't get crazier than that."

Linc looked back at him. There had been a time, he recalled, when he had looked upon Chips as "cool"—the way to be in maybe another year's time. Now he saw just a kid with a loud mouth, who wore a hat that was too big and a cheap suit that needed pressing. Another Kyle in the making. He would cause a lot of people trouble and grief—and very possibly die suddenly because he didn't have the brains to know his limits and would get overambitious. Linc could pretty much guess the fates mapped out for the others too. Larry would kick down the wrong door one day and walk into a shotgun blast coming the other way. And although he knew nothing about them, he could already read a repeat performance of the Clay-and-Slam act in Gomez and Lou, destined to go down the same tubes. In Joe alone he sensed a potential that the right opportunity could maybe bring to bud and make flower.

But there was no way Linc would change any of that now, any more than he was about to bring a new crusade to the world. There was really only one other thing he wanted to know. He had decided to try and get news first, rather than walk in cold to any ugly surprises. "I'll be stopping by to see my folks later," he said, forcing his voice to remain casual. "How have they been doing? Is everything okay with them as far as you guys know?"

Chips looked at Joe and Larry as if it were an odd question to be asked, and spread his hands. "Sure, as far as I know. Did you guys hear any different?" They shook their heads. "That sister of yours was in Dobe's, oh, a week or two back," Chips told Linc. "What's her name? . . . The one who was shacked up with that jerk you worked over once."

"Marcella," Joe put in.

"She's not with him now, then?" Linc checked.

Chips shook his head. "Nah. He was feeling heat and blew town. I don't know the details. But if there were any problems at home, she'd have said." He looked to the others for confirmation. They nodded. "Sure, she'd have said," he repeated.

Linc felt relieved. At least whoever sent Sammy with the message after Linc was arrested had played straight on that score and not seen reason to carry out their threat.

There was nothing more to be accomplished here. Linc pushed back his chair and stood up. "Well, I've got things to do, and there's only today. Take care, you guys. Don't go walking into any trucks. And, who knows, maybe I'll be back and stop in again one day, eh?"

"You going already?" Chips said. "You've only just sat down."

"It's like I said—lots to do, not a lot of time."

"Well, okay. . . . And hey, glad you made it, anyhow."

Larry looked at Linc expressionlessly. Joe mustered a grin and offered a hand. "Good luck out there, Linc," he said. "I never thought I'd see the day you got religion, man."

"It's not exactly the way you think," Linc told him.

Lou just nodded. Gomez stared at Linc sourly.

On his way out through the front of the restaurant, Linc stopped Dino's niece, Carla, who was working the tables. "Hey, remember me?"

Carla stared back at him for a second, then her eyes widened. "Linc! You're back! Why didn't anybody tell me?"

"Because they didn't know. So how's everything?"

"Oh, you know. . . ." She shrugged. "It's like the weather, some days up, some down. And you?"

"Just fine. Look, I'm in a bit of a hurry, so I can't explain, but I want you to do something for me."

"Well, sure . . . if I can."

Linc took out his pocket phone and handed it to her. "Wait about a half a minute, then take this out back and give it to Joe—you know, the guy with the hair tied back. . . ."

"Yes, Joe Baloney. I know."

"Tell him I dropped it on the way out. I'm heading uptown." Linc saw the frown and questions already starting to form. "I don't have time. Just do it," he said.

Joe caught him a couple of minutes later, when Linc just happened to have stopped to look in the window of an electronics shop. "Linc, is this yours? Carla gave it to me. She said you dropped it."

Linc turned and took the phone. "Thanks." Joe looked puzzled at Linc's evident lack of surprise. "No, I gave it to her," Linc said. "I wanted to talk to you away from those other guys. Look, give me your call code and a mail drop, would you?"

Joe's puzzlement increased, but he complied. Linc keyed the details into the phone's scratch memory. "Sometime later, I don't know exactly when, someone will contact you and mention my name," he said. "When they do, listen carefully to what they tell you. It will be *very* important, Joe—maybe involving one of the most important decisions you'll ever make in your life."

CHAPTER THIRTY-SIX

NOTHING had changed much in the house. Cartons of empties and bags of trash waiting to be put out were still piled behind the kitchen door. The tacky, coming-apart couch had been replaced by a just-as-tacky couch that looked as if it wouldn't be long coming apart. There was a new, wall-size TV with VR console, probably not a button on it yet paid for.

Linc's father looked paler than he remembered, the flesh under his eyes more saggy. Although it was afternoon, he was still in a coffee-stained undershirt and hadn't shaved. Linc's mother, in a robe and smoking a cigarette, was puffy-faced and hungover, half spaced on something that was supposed to take care of it—probably other things as well. She had shown no more reaction to Linc's appearance than if he had returned from going to the grocery store along the street half an hour ago. Linc had given up attempting to explain the Outzone and what it meant. Their perceptions had been shaped by media depictions, which Linc now had no doubt were contrived deliberately to mislead and misinform. Linc's father was relieved that Linc seemed to be straightening out, but couldn't get it out of his head that what Linc would be going back to was a correctional program run by the government. "I didn't know they had places out there that they sent people to," was the only comment Linc had been able to evince.

"Did you ever hear from Sadie?" Linc asked them. His father had offered him a beer, but he'd preferred coffee. They were out of it, but his mother had found some instant in an old jar at the back of a shelf, and he had made himself one in a plastic mug and brought it back out. It was bitter, watery, but drinkable.

"We get E-mails every now and again," his mother said. She looked across at Linc's father. "Where was she last time? . . ."

"I'm not sure. Someplace in California, wasn't it?"

"Oh, you don't know anything. What was she doing there?"

"She met up with some guy who breaks up cars and deals in parts," Linc's father answered. "Somewhere around Sacramento, I think she said."

"What happened to that guy she took off from here with?" Linc asked. "The big wheeler-dealer with the used Honda, who was gonna buy her the world."

"Honda? . . . I don't remember him," Linc's mother said. "Who's Honda? Do we have a drink anywhere around here?"

"Let's save it for a while huh? Linc's only just back."

"Damn it, I want a drink."

"I heard Marcella was around last week," Linc said.

His father nodded. "Yes, she's back staying here for a while—using your old room. . . . Is that okay? It seemed a shame not to, when it was there empty. And she had all this stuff—"

Linc held up a hand. "It doesn't matter. Sure, it's okay."

His father nodded but went on anyway, "It's just that there was this big fight with that guy she went with—you know, the one you went over and beat up once—and she didn't want to be out there on her own. He turned out to be really strange, you know—like anything could happen. It seems you were right about him."

"So long as she's okay now," Linc said. "So what's she doing? Has she got herself some kind of job?"

His father shook his head. "I don't ask. She helps out big with the rent and the bills. That's good enough."

"Wasn't Honda the one who said he knew people in movies?" Linc's mother said suddenly, coming back briefly from wherever her reveries had taken her. Linc and his father waited a few moments.

"Who told you Marcella was around?" Linc's father asked.

"Oh, I talked to some of the guys already."

"Nobody's listening. I'll get it myself." His mother got up and went back through to the kitchen. The sounds came back of a closet door banging and ice falling into a glass.

"She'll be back later tonight. You'll be able to see her then," Linc's father said.

Linc shook his head. "Sorry, but I won't be staying. I have some friends waiting across town that I have to meet. We're shipping back up in three days. I just wanted to stop by. But tell her I was asking, that I'm doing just fine, and to take care, okay?"

"Oh. . . . You won't be able to stay even that long, huh? That's too bad. I was hoping maybe . . ." Linc's father frowned, and the words ran out. He didn't seem too sure of just what he'd been hoping. "Well, I guess if you have to get back, you have to get back. Kinda like a parole is it? You have to be back when they say or it messes up your record." Linc sighed and said nothing.

His mother shuffled back in with her drink, sat down again, and lit another cigarette. "Isn't *The Celia Show* supposed to be on now?" she said.

"Linc's only just back. He'll be going again soon."

Linc looked at them. There were a hundred other things

that he could have talked about. But what would be the point of even trying? He finished his coffee, put down the plastic mug, and stood up.

"Oh, you're leaving now?" His father stood up and hovered anxiously.

"You know how it is." Linc looked at them again and thought for a moment. "There are a couple of things in my room I need to check. It won't take a second."

"Sure—go ahead. We didn't move any of your things out. Everything's all there. . . . We will be hearing from you again, won't we?"

"Yes, but I'm not sure when. It might be a while," Linc said as he left the room.

"He's going already?" his mother's voice said behind him. "We can put the show on then."

Marcella had draped a lot of frilly things and lacy things around the room, and strewn fluffy cushions on the bed. The chest of drawers had been pushed back into a corner to make room for a vanity, which was covered with makeup bottles and jars. Movie-star pictures had been added to the walls, along with a couple of airline posters, one showing Norway, the other, Argentina; also, interestingly, set on its own as if in a place of special honor, there was a framed photo of Linc.

He moved over to the closet and opened it to reveal a colorful selection of dresses, skirts, coats, slacks, and jeans, with belts and purses hanging inside the door and a jumble of shoes on the floor. His own clothes were still there, pushed back to the far end of the rail. He ruffled through them curiously. They reminded him of Chips—loud and flashy; a kid's attempt at copying something he didn't understand. Funny how Chips was two years older and couldn't yet see what was now so plain to Linc. . . . But then, no. It wasn't funny at all. Chips never would see it.

Linc went down on one knee and lifted aside his own shoes at the rear. He took a quarter from his pocket and used it to pry away the section of the baseboard covering a recess at the bottom of the wall he had cut long ago. He felt inside and drew out a large, brown envelope, folded in half and bound with rubber bands. He opened it and pulled out the wads of fifties and hundreds from inside.

Almost nine thousand dollars. That was to have been the down payment for the car he was going to have like Kyle's when he reached driving age, along with the suit and other accessories to pull the broad to go with it. It was all there, untouched. He counted off a few and pocketed them to take care of the next couple of days, then put the rest back in the envelope and replaced the cover on the recess. Then he straightened up and went back through to the living room.

His father took the package unresistingly when Linc pressed it into his hand. "This is for you . . . for everything. It should help out with a lot of things," Linc said. "I have to go. Tell Marcella I'm sorry I couldn't stay. The room looks really nice. I'll be in touch from time to time to make sure everything's okay."

Linc left the house and used his pocket phone to call a cab. One appeared, coming along by the river, just as he reached the end of the street.

Julie was with Arvin and Marlene in the hotel coffee shop and bar where they had arranged to meet on the other side of town. Going back home and to his old haunts had been something Linc wanted to do alone.

Another advantage in having Arvin along had been not having to leave the two girls on their own. Arvin had chosen to wear his uniform, which being unusual had attracted some attention, and by the time Linc arrived his three companions had become the center of quite a party of interested people.

Arvin had obviously told the story of the accident at Grayling. "This is the guy!" he exclaimed when Linc walked in through the door from the street. "He's the one. If he hadn't done what he did, I wouldn't be here talking to you now."

An enemy had become a friend that Linc would keep for life. And in realizing that, Linc finally grasped what his education had been about. By the values that held in the Outzone, he was already rich. Now, at last, he understood the form of wealth the new civilization would be built on.

They had dinner, and Linc treated them all to a show. The next day Rocky and Liz joined them. Two days of relaxation followed. Then came the flight back to Yucatán and the routine of being checked once more onto one of the outbound shuttles. The daylong lift up and around the Moon was exciting but uneventful. When they docked at Grayling Station, the *Neil A. Armstrong* was already in orbit standing twelve miles off and had begun preparations for departure.

CHAPTER THIRTY-SEVEN

ON reporting to Captain Ullerman, Linc learned that Colonel Weyer had asked to be notified immediately when Linc returned. Captain Ullerman called Colonel Weyer's office and was informed that the colonel would like to see him and Linc there. After going off the line to check, the adjutant Captain Ullerman had spoken to called back to say they were scheduled into a slot just over an hour later. Linc went away to clean up and change after his journey. Then he used the time to collect together his kit and other belongings in the billet in readiness for moving out. The senior cadets bantered while they packed and tried to act nonchalantly in an effort to hide the nervousness tearing them apart inside, while the rookies who wouldn't be going watched enviously. Linc remembered how it had felt. But at least they would be getting a stripe.

Only one person was with the colonel this time when Linc and Captain Ullerman were shown into Colonel Weyer's office: an officer in a uniform similar to those worn by Grayling crew but with an altered cut to the collar and different insignia. Colonel Weyer introduced him as Captain Seyger from the flight engineering crew of the *Armstrong*.

Obviously, Linc was told, with all that was going on, there wasn't time now to change the administrative arrangements concerning him that presently stood. This came as no surprise. It had never occurred to Linc that anyone would think there might be a way to alter things. The proposal put to him was that after arrival at the Outzone, he would be offered the option of going into the Fleet Engineering School as a technician apprentice. The training he would get there would provide a background that could lead later to a broad range of skilled professions in such areas as development and construction, repair, or maintenance in any of the space-borne or surface bases coming into existence all over the Outzone, or as spaceflight crew. Alternatively, he could remain with the military and transfer into one of the technical branches, again with a range of possible space-going or base-oriented futures. The voyage out would give him time to think it over. Captain Seyger would be available during the voyage to answer any questions.

Linc was too overwhelmed to think of anything much to ask just then. The only question that came immediately to mind was, "What difference will it make to where I go after we get there?"

"None at all, to begin with," Colonel Weyer replied. "Practically all new arrivals are processed through Coombe, on Callisto, which is becoming a miniature city these days. They do their first three months adapting and acclimatizing there before going on to the destiny they've got planned—or whatever fate has in store for them."

"Er, I was really thinking about after that . . ." Linc wasn't sure if it was appropriate to bring the topic up and looked at Captain Ullerman questioningly.

"I think Cadet Marani is concerned about his young lady, sir," Captain Ullerman said.

"Ah, yes . . . nurse's orderly Yeats." The colonel's eyes twinkled for a moment. "Medical trainees normally go through their introductory phase at Coombe too, of course. As to after that . . . well, you may rest assured that the powers that be will do their best to accommodate such preferences as you have indicated. Fair enough, young man?"

"Fair enough, sir," Linc agreed. Captain Ullerman winked at him. It would be okay.

And so, after bidding farewells to friends and making all the usual pledges to stay in touch and get together again when they were next in the same place, Linc and his group found themselves hoisting kit bags and tramping for the last time through the lime-green metal corridors that had become, in a way, a strange kind of home. They took the conveyor elevator to the Axle, where there were officially checked out of Grayling Station. Forty minutes later a personnel carrier detached to ferry them across to the waiting ship.

CHAPTER THIRTY-EIGHT

"WE *have ten minutes to burn, and counting.*"

This time Linc was hearing the words from a bench seat in the Aft Personnel Lounge on C Deck, inside the *Neil A. Armstrong*. He reached out to Julie, sitting next to him, and gave her arm a quick squeeze. Opposite them, Arvin and Flash made okay signs at each other. Patch, from Coulie days, was with them again, having reappeared just in time to catch the ship. He had been in Alaska, going through an intensive course in mountaineering and survival as a preparation for surface training on the Jovian moons. The intention was that he would go on to specialize in survey and prospecting work. So perhaps he and Linc wouldn't have to wait until they were back on Earth to go climbing together again after all—if tackling ice slopes against a quarter of Earth's gravity could be called climbing.

The views alternating on the screen were similar to before: the ship hanging in space, now bereft of its gaggle of service vessels; Grayling, turning amid its scattered formation of outstations; *Sysiphus* on its way around the Moon, trailing down its line. Linc remembered how, as he watched these images before, he had thought about the people out there inside the ship, trying to imagine how they must be feeling as they waited through the final moments. Now he was one of them.

"Eight minutes. The hook is on target."

"If you've got any second thoughts now, you might as well forget 'em." Johnny "Piano Man" flashed one of his smiles. He had reappeared too, after being spirited away to meet people he hadn't cared to name and taking a course in political science. Apparently a lot of things that were "subversive" on Earth were considered worth listening to in the Outzone.

"Any second thoughts?" Linc asked Julie.

She smiled and shook her head.

And Big Mac was back from a college stint also, his sights set on the design side of construction engineering. He had been in touch with Mace, who was already at Coombe and said life there was hectic but great. The sight of Jupiter in the night sky was "awesome," Mace had told him. "Like all the sunsets you ever saw, rolled together into one big ball."

"Seven minutes."

The view switched to a shot of the *Armstrong*'s drive nozzles. Willie, a short distance away with Mackerel, Arch, Gus, and several of the others, pointed at the screen while he said something—probably giving one of his technical commentaries. Linc was happy not to have to listen. From Coombe, Willie would almost certainly be routed on to Ganymede, which was where military pilots went through training. Ganymede seemed to be the center of the Outzone's military activities. If Linc elected to remain with the service, it was likely he would be sent there for a stretch too.

"Okay, guys, what are you gonna miss the most?" Arvin asked the others.

Big Mac answered first. "Sunshine and beaches. Real sun—you know, near enough to make rocks fry eggs."

"I thought you said that Mace told you they're making one at Coombe," Flash said.

"Yeah, sure. Inside a dome with artificial sand, with a plasma ball and a machine that has to make the waves. Sorry, but for me that's not a mark on the plus side."

"It might be, six months from now," Flash suggested.

"For me, oh, I dunno. . . . Just knowing the rest of the world's out there, I guess," Johnny told them. "You know—that more planets exist between the bus stops."

"What I'm gonna miss is real mountains," Patch said. "Boy, you should have seen some of these places in Alaska, Linc! We have to go back there sometime."

They all looked at Linc questioningly. He thought for a few seconds, asking himself what he would miss the most. Finally, he shrugged. "Nothing much."

"Five minutes and counting. Plasma and fields all in spec, and hook in the window. Five-zero proceed order confirmed."

A local announcement followed from inside the ship. "It looks like we're on our way, folks. Stewards check that everyone is seated and secured. The g force will be less than you're used to on a regular airplane, but it's not a time for people to be milling around. The good ship *Neil A. Armstrong*, about to depart for Callisto. If you don't want to go to Callisto, don't waste your time telling us now. Well, we're going to be busy up front for some time. Talk to you again later when we're under way."

Once again, Linc found himself watching a numeric superposition at the top of the screen. *04:15 . . . 04:14 . . .*

"For me, what I'll miss is being able to play a decent ball game," Arvin said. "I mean, how could you make it work? The gravity and everything would make it all different. Did Mace say anything about that?"

Big Mac shook his head. "I never thought to ask him."

"Willie'll know," Flash said. He called along to the next bay of seats, "Hey, Willie, how do you play baseball on Callisto?"

"What's baseball?" Willie threw back.

Arvin groaned, shook his head and covered his eyes.

"Three minutes. . . ."

Like a replay of before, the screen showed the inside of the Grayling Bridge with the crew stations manned, Kelsoe at the main panel, flanked by his EO and the CEO. Then came the shot from *Sisyphus* showing the tether line curving upward—from the perspective of its surface station—and away into space.

"I feel like a trout waiting to be jerked out of the water," Big Mac said. He was new in space compared with most of them, and so found it all doubly traumatic. Not only was this the first orbital liftout he'd seen; he would be going with it.

"You won't even feel it," Linc told him. "Like it just said, the g's less than when you take off in a plane."

"And we power up to match it," Flash added—needlessly, really, since they had all been briefed on the drill. As happened to almost everyone, he was seizing on anything to talk about as the zero hour approached.

"Two minutes to burn, and counting. . . ."

Linc found that he didn't feel like saying anything. His mind went back to streets and the life he had grown up in, all those years knowing of nothing else, and then the strange combinations of circumstances that had resulted in bringing him to where he was now. He thought of the billions of people scattered across the world, and what the total of what they were capable of doing and knowing could add up to. The ability was there to turn any dream that they wanted into reality. They could create what he had seen out here, and the things he would be going to; or they could be devoured by the things he was leaving behind—all of it creations of none but themselves. But even if all of them had the chance to choose as he had, how many would have? . . .

"Hey, Linc, anyone there?" Johnny's voice brought him back. "You look like you're halfway to Jupiter already." Linc grinned tiredly.

"Oh, no, he's right here," Julie said, clutching his arm.

"One minute. Deployment good. Sequence to auto."

"All crew to station."

Linc felt his pulse rate rising and strange tingles racing down his spine as the same words he had heard before replayed themselves:

"Plasma primaries are at heat, and go."

"Injection fields are go."

"Attitude and profile check positive function."

A cut to Grayling's Bridge again, Kelsoe and the CEO.

"We have go at zero minus thirty-eight seconds. Drive initialization syncing now."

Movement and the pretenses of normality all around had ceased. Everyone stared at the screen showing the view of the ship from one of the service craft. Linc felt Julie's fingers tightening around his arm.

00:05 . . . 00:04 . . . 00:03 . . . 00:02 . . . 00:01. . . .

On the screen a torch of light leaped out from the *Armstrong* and seared across space.

"Injection. . . . Plasma ignition. . . . Acceleration registering . . . We have liftout!"

They watched the ship beginning to move against the stars and at the same time felt it as a mild urging transmitted through the floor and the seats. The image on the screen gained speed and foreshortened, but the sensation inside was unchanged. Only when the view switched to a rear view from the *Armstrong* showing Grayling Station and its satellites already as points vanishing into the distance was there a real indication of how fast they were already moving.

"Sisyphus is coming overhead. . . . Lineup is good. . . . Connecting now." The view changed to the grab line from the ship extending upward, and another line from off the screen in the final stages of close. *"Tension. . . . We are under boost."*

The sensation of weight increased noticeably but not violently. Nevertheless, Linc knew that their acceleration was almost doubled, slinging the ship into a course that would take it on its way out from Earth and across the solar system.

The Moon slid in toward the center of the screen, already smaller than seen from Grayling. Then, as the *Armstrong* swung outward and upward under the combined impulse of its engines and the momentum being returned through the tether, Earth began showing on one side of it. Linc remembered how he had looked down across California's great Central Valley from a peak in the Sierra and pictured the invisible people scurrying below, lost in their tiny worlds of imaginary worries and self-inflicted problems, unaware of the different reality that was within their grasp and so close, if they would only lift their heads to see it. Now he thought it about the whole world.

And yet, somewhere down there beneath those clouds another group, even now as he watched, would be going through Coulie, who would follow. And one day in the city, somebody would seek out Joe, and there would be other Joes from other cities, and they would follow too. Linc wondered how many others had watched such a view of Earth from an outgoing ship and thought similar things, long before Linc had even known Coulie existed. Before much longer now, he would meet them.

"At the high point and on target. Letting go the line. We are now on course for Jupiter. Launch crew can stand down."

The ship had become a free creature, soaring outward toward the distant point of light that would grow and take on color and form as the days passed by. Shouts of jubilation, laughs, smiles, back slappings and a few tears broke out around the deck as all the pent-up tensions dissipated. Linc and Julie found each other's hands and clutched tightly. They would doubtless return to Earth in the years to come and probably find themselves leaving it again, maybe many times. But never again could it quite be like this. They both tried to find words to say what they felt just at that moment, but there were none. Everyone else seemed to be having the same problem.

On the screen a last view being transmitted from somewhere near the Moon showed the ship as a haze of white, already diminishing among the stars.